# HE DESERVED TO DIE

Anna Ruth Worten-Fritz

Fulton Books, Inc.
Meadville, PA

Published by Fulton Books 2021

ISBN 978-1-63860-877-6 (paperback)
ISBN 978-1-63860-878-3 (digital)

Printed in the United States of America

For my Old Sames, my Yayas,
my family,
my Indian sister,
my favorite candy striper,
and for Old Folks Talking,
all quite the characters.

## CHAPTER 1

# ANTHONY GRASSO

*6:20 a.m., the morning of the killing*
*Anthony's driveway*

*Ffffft.* Stunned by the unexpected shot fired, Anthony froze, unable to breathe and unable to speak. As his body lurched forward, he could hear his face shatter when it crashed onto the steel hitch of the motorcycle trailer he was attempting to release moments earlier. His head was contorted upward, in an unnatural position, but there was nothing he could do to right this. He agonized but did not have the strength to dislodge himself off the metal trailer hitch.

The fumes of the F250 gagged him. He hadn't bothered to shut off the engine. It was only going to take a minute to release the trailer so he could pull his truck into the garage.

His vision blurred. Anthony tried to gather his thoughts.

*What just happened?*

Unable to move, he could just take in his limited field of vision by pivoting his eyes. To his left, the viburnum he planted seventeen years ago with his first wife was as thick as a wall. There was no way to see beyond that.

Gravity suddenly won out. His head was released from the trailer with a loud thump. He collapsed between the trailer and the truck in a second wave of excruciating pain as he smashed the neatly bricked driveway teeth first.

The early morning darkness obscured his view of the perpetrator.

*Someone finally got the moxy to follow through with one of the many threats I've received over the years,* he thought to himself in a panic.

From the new angle, he could make out the sneakers pointed directly at him, right under the streetlamp where the two driveways met, punctuated by both mailboxes. Just within a few feet from him, at the end of his driveway, he recognized his killer.

*The fool!* he wanted to scream, but nothing actually escaped from his mouth.

His body throbbed where the shot pierced his heart. The pain stole his voice. He could feel his blood and his life drain slowly away.

Hope came in the form of a loud engine rev. A large vehicle roared onto the street, possibly the garbage men he fought with each week.

*Those jerks would have to stop. They'll have to notice the blood spreading down the pavers. They'll find me. They'll save me.* Hope soon faded as he realized, *No, today is Monday. Garbage day isn't until tomorrow.*

The noisy school bus lumbered past his nearly lifeless body, unnoticed. In the dark, he became aware of the other figure staring, watching in the shadows as his life slipped away from him, just beyond the reach of the streetlamp.

A new flicker of hope emerged, a loud, confusing thumping.

# CHAPTER 2

# 911

*7:00 a.m., the morning of the killing*
*Emergency phone operator*

"911, what's your emergency?"

"Oh my god! There's a man lying in a pool of blood. I think he's dead."

"We are going to send help. Where are you located?"

"Um, I…uh…on Blessed Lane. Sorry, I can't think straight." She began to sob. "I just moved in. No, it is Blessed Drive," she corrected herself. "I am at the second to last house on Blessed Drive next to Lake Harmony in South Shore. I don't know his specific address."

"Calm down, ma'am. I am going to remain on the line. I have sent help for you. Does the man have a pulse?"

"Hold on. Let me check."

The phone clanked to the ground. The sounds were muffled as if it were dropped rather than gently placed down. After a moment of empty air time, the frazzled voice returned.

"No, there is no pulse! I couldn't find his pulse! I am sure he is dead. There's a tremendous amount of blood. It's everywhere, all over the ground!"

Then a despondent weep whimpered into the phone, followed by several gasps for air and sniffles as the woman tried to steady herself, unaccustomed to death and dying.

"May I ask your name, please?"

The 911 operator used her most soothing voice to help calm the Good Samaritan.

"I am Nita Washington. I just moved into the house across the street."

"Do you know who the man is?"

The well-trained operator kept the woman on the line, collecting as much information as she could until the police arrived.

"I'm not certain, but I think it is my neighbor. At least it is my neighbor's house."

Mrs. Washington worked herself up again, releasing another sob before taking several deep breaths, trying to regain her composure once more.

"There is no one else around. My husband has gone to work already. The neighbors are gone too. I am here all by myself."

"You are not alone. I will stay with you until help arrives. I have already sent someone, and they will arrive any minute now. Where is the blood coming from?"

"He is facedown and kind of in a hovel under his truck. I didn't want to move him. And it is still kind of dark out. But his shirt is soaked in blood. I think it is his chest or maybe torso. I think he was shot in his chest. Oh, wait, I see blue-and-red lights reflecting off the stop sign. No sirens, but it is definitely the police."

"Okay, you did a great job by calling in the emergency and identifying the location. You can let the police take over from here."

"Thank you for staying with me."

"You're in good hands now. You're most welcome. We are always here to assist."

Mrs. Washington hung up the phone with the flick of her thumb and turned her attention to the responding police officers exiting their vehicle. The police car parked on the road between her neighbor's home and her own, faced in the wrong direction. Nita sensed a huge relief when she saw it was a Black female officer that stepped out of the police car first. The officer was speaking into the radio on her shoulder as she walked toward the crumpled victim. Nita made no attempt to wipe away her tears.

CHAPTER 3

# DETECTIVE DON HANNON

*7:45 a.m., the morning of the killing*
*South Shore neighborhood*

*I love this neighborhood,* Detective Hannon thought to himself as he turned into South Shore.

It looked like it should have been a gated community, but there was no gate necessary here because it was developed around Lake Harmony, out in the sticks, in the middle of nowhere.

Detective Hannon dreamed one day of owning his own house in this neighborhood. The yards were well landscaped, and it was unlike any of the other subdivisions in Harmony. The four builders had agreed seventeen years ago to not take down any trees unnecessarily. No fences were permitted either. If a homeowner wanted a divider, it would have to be a natural barrier such as bushes, trees, or uncut natural vegetation.

Because the economy was so sleepy in this area, many of the lots had not sold, and so the woods remained untouched. Nightly and in the early morning hours of dawn, wildlife emerged unmolested by their human neighbors. Deer grazed in the yards. Rabbits peeked out of the palmetto bushes in every single manicured lawn. Sandhill cranes poked holes, which disturbed the otherwise well-groomed St. Augustine grass.

There were plenty of places for children to play and hide. There were plenty of places for criminals to play and hide.

As he took his first left on Blessed Drive, the long street bent right, and he could now easily see the strobing blue-and-red lights in the full morning sunlight emerge. The reflection from street signs bounced the lights from his rearview mirror, which gave the effect of double the police presence.

The name Blessed Drive seemed somewhat ironic considering the circumstances that brought him here. The ten-foot-tall bushes that divided the corpse from his only next-door neighbor made it impossible to see the neighbor's house unless you were standing directly in front of it. The full block was one mile in circumference. The house across the street was recessed back into the woods. The next closest neighbor's home was isolated by the natural bush, close in proximity but impossible to see from the street view or from the victim's driveway. Possibly fifty or sixty feet lie from the front door to the end of the driveway.

Behind the victim's home was one thousand acres of preserve. Lake Harmony Preserve had an extensive equestrian trail. The Boy Scouts used the preserve for geocaching, a high-tech hide-and-seek game in which they used a GPS to locate various caches of assorted items including a logbook.

The next closest house from the victim's home was down the street, from the way he had come, probably four or five lots away if homes had actually been built yet. At the very end of the street, two wooded lots past the victim's neighbor's home, was a neighborhood dock that buttressed into Lake Harmony. The only landing available to launch a boat in Lake Harmony. Only South Shore residents possessed the key for the boat ramp. So this very secluded area didn't have the usual lookie-loos.

With a worried and stressed look about her, a dark-skinned woman in her early forties was standing in her robe and nightgown, speaking with Detective Pontonero when he pulled onto the crime scene.

"Good morning, ma'am."

Hannon noticed right away the blood on her right hand and the sleeve of her bathrobe.

"Well, it has been a morning. I would not describe it as good though," Mrs. Washington replied without any sense of sarcasm.

"This is Nita Washington. Mrs. Washington found the body and reported it to the emergency operator this morning around 7:00 a.m.," Pontonero offered the introductions.

"Hello, Ms. Washington, I am Detective Hannon with the St. Cloud Police Department."

He did not extend his hand. No need to unnecessarily dirty his own hand.

"I'd like to ask you a few questions later, after I speak to my partner. Would that be all right with you?"

"Yes, of course. I don't have any place I have to be. But I already told Detective Pontonero everything I know."

"Just to be thorough, ma'am."

"Detective Pontonero, have you used the Instant Shooter Identification Kit yet with Mrs. Washington?"

This is a portable device the detectives use to determine if someone has fired a gun recently. The electrode did not, in fact, pick up on any GSR, or gunshot residue, on Nita Washington's hands.

"I have, and she's clean, so to speak," he answered, smiling at Mrs. Washington as if thanking her for tolerating the indignity.

"You can go back inside now and get cleaned up. We know where you are when we need you."

Shaken by the events of the morning and eager to wash away the blood, Mrs. Washington gladly headed back to her own home for a long, warm bubble bath.

"Okay, Pont, what do we know?"

"What, no coffee from *Sip and Dip*?" Pont quipped.

"It was your turn to bring the coffee," Hannon retorted.

"Well, it looks like our vic was trying to unhitch his truck from his trailer when he was ambushed from the side."

He pointed to the woods across the street, adjacent to Mr. and Mrs. Washington's new home.

"The entrance wound is here."

He pointed to the small hole on the victim's left side.

"And the exit wound is quite a bit larger here," he said, indicating the right side of the torso. "So the shot came from the direction of the woods toward the preserve, not the other way around. His F250 was still running when I arrived. Mrs. Washington noticed it running when she found the body, but she said she didn't want to disturb anything."

Looking across the street as the young woman entered her own foyer, Detective Hannon wondered out loud, "How did she even see the body from this angle behind the big cargo trailer and the wall of bushes?"

"Well, she didn't at first. She and her husband just moved into the neighborhood. Her husband, Darius Washington, was hired as the new head football coach at Harmony High School."

"Oh yeah, I just read about him in the gazette. Go Longhorns. From the write-up in the article, it looks like we are finally going to have a winning season."

Pontonero pulled a strange face at Detective Hannon.

"Well, anyway, she reported that she had breakfast with her husband, Darius, and after he went to work, Mrs. Washington was dragging out some of the empty boxes from the recent move. She mentioned that each time, she noticed the truck was running with the door ajar, and the door chimes continued to sound with the lights still on in the cabin. And the trailer lights and the headlights were left on too. On her third trip or so, out to the curb, it started getting lighter out, so she took a closer look to see what was going on. That's when she noticed the patterns the blood made along the seams of the pavers and in the change of color where the sidewalk intersects the pavers. She walked around the front of the truck. Upon closer inspection, and by the smell, she determined it was blood. She discovered the body under the truck. It looks like the tongue of the hitch did a pretty good hit job on his face. His teeth are smashed in," Pont described.

"Oh, nice. I am going to have sweet dreams tonight," Detective Hannon bantered.

"We found $500 in cash in his wallet. His ID says he is Anthony Grasso, forty-nine years old. This is his home, according to the address on his driver's license," Pont continued.

"Why did Mrs. Washington have blood on her robe and her hand if she didn't want to disturb anything?"

"I asked her that very same question, Don. Apparently, the 911 operator asked her to feel for Mr. Grasso's pulse. And as you can see, she found none."

"Where is the weapon?"

"That's the thing. There is no weapon. No evidence anywhere that we can find. No bullets, no gun, no robbery. No bullet marks on the garage, in the garage, or in the walls. It could have gone straight back into the backyard and beyond, into the woods, I suppose."

"Has everything been photographed yet?" Hannon inquired.

"Yeah," Pont replied. "We will have to have forensics look at the truck closely to see if they find something lodged into the truck."

"Could it be an ill-aimed hunter poaching the preserve?" Detective Pontonero considered.

After a moment's reflection, "Possibly...let's hope so. The forensic team will be able to determine that. For now, we are investigating it as a homicide."

"The neighbor is trying to get past our crime scene," Detective Pontonero observed.

"Go talk to her and canvass the rest of the neighbors. I will look around here some more and notify the family. Let's meet up for lunch around noon at *Meat n Fire* and go over our findings."

# CHAPTER 4

# JOYCE KRAUS

*Five days before the killing*
*At the Washington's front door*

"Just knock one more time," Joyce whispered to her daughter, Natalie.

Slowly an eyeball peeked out from behind a barely cracked door. "May I help you?" a soft, lilting voice answered.

Loudly, Natalie practically shouted from excitement. "We made you brownies!"

This time, the door fully opened wide, and a beautiful young woman emerged in a yoga bra and yoga pants with her hair bunched up in a topknot on the center of her head. Her caramel-colored skin was glowing with sweat.

"Oh, sorry, did we disturb you from your exercise?" Joyce questioned apologetically.

"No, no. I was just organizing boxes and unpacking. Please forgive my appearance. I wasn't expecting any company."

"Hi," Joyce said, extending her arm to shake her hand, "I am Joyce Kraus, and this is my daughter, Natalie. We wanted to welcome you to the neighborhood and drop off a treat. We don't want to keep you from your work."

"Why, thank you, I'm pleased to make your acquaintance," she said, graciously extending her hand to receive the handshake and then to receive the brownies.

She stepped out further, with more confidence, onto the wide-open front porch.

"I am Nita Washington. My husband, Darius, hasn't come home from work yet. He's still at football practice."

"My son, Reed, and his friends told us all about Coach Washington. He is quite excited for a new season with a new coach. The whole town really is expecting big results this year."

"Does Reed play football?" Nita returned the pleasantries.

"Not this year, but he did his freshman year on the junior varsity team. He is taking a lot of advanced placement classes, so he is going to focus on his academics this year. Most of his buddies play football though. You know well how much time football requires. It is quite a commitment at the high school level. My husband, Ron, gave Reed a choice of either hunting or football, and Reed chose hunting. Between you and me, I think Ron nudged him in that direction a little," Mrs. Kraus gave Nita a knowing wink.

"I would invite you in, but the house is still chaotic. There really is no place for you to sit yet," Nita said, pointing inside to the kitchen. "Your brownies look delicious. Would you like me to cut you a piece?"

"Yes, please!" Natalie squealed in excitement.

Joyce laughed sympathetically but shook her head.

"No, sweetheart, they are for Nita and her husband. We can make some more for our family later."

"I really don't mind. It is just me and Darius, and he is really into fitness. He doesn't touch any sweets. I, however, love anything chocolate, but I can't eat the whole pan by myself."

Her reasoning made sense, but Joyce was not about to take back part of her gift despite her daughter clearly wanting the delicious warm brownie.

"We know that you are busy. We just wanted to welcome you to the neighborhood and let you know that if you need anything, we are right across the street and happy to help."

"Well, thank you."

Mrs. Washington changed her voice into more of a whisper.

"To be honest, I wasn't going to answer the door. The first welcoming party wasn't so welcoming."

"Oh no, please don't tell me 'Mr. Happy' said something nasty to you."

"Well, if 'Mr. Happy' is the racist jerk across the street, yeah, he said something to us all right. He actually called us the N-word to our face."

Joyce took a step back. "You have got to be kidding me!" Joyce gaped her mouth open in disbelief.

Natalie was even offended. "That is a bad word. I would never ever use that word."

Nita smiled at the sweet girl in appreciation for her solidarity.

"What did you and Darius do?" Before Nita had time to respond to the first question, she asked the second, "What did you say to that jerk?"

"Darius told me to go into the house. So I did. I was so terrified that I almost called the police. From the window, I watched Darius walk up to that fascist neo-Nazi. Darius put his face an inch from his nose, and whatever he said made the bully turn right around and walk back across the street."

"Oh my gosh, I am so sorry this happened to you too."

Sincerity was conveyed.

Nita's brow furrowed. "What do you mean happened to you *too*?"

With a deep inhale, Joyce relayed the unfortunate story of the previous owners.

"Anthony is a bigot and misogynist. He is simply the worst racist you will ever meet. He chased off the previous neighbors, Mr. and Mrs. Sundaram. They were a very nice elderly couple from India."

Mrs. Kraus shifted her weight and placed her hand on her hip, settling into the story.

"Like most bullies, Mr. Happy would have backed down if confronted. But the Sundarams were devout pacifists. He intimidated them daily. Mrs. Sundaram confided in me that her husband was having health issues because of the stress Anthony was putting him under."

Mrs. Kraus placed her hand on Natalie's shoulder to give her comfort. She knew this conversation made Natalie very uncomfortable.

"The poor couple had to sell their restaurant, the only Indian restaurant for miles around here. It was such a cool restaurant. They served food family style, the big round tables with the lazy Susan in the center of the table that turned the food to you. All the female servers wore brightly colored saris, and the male servers wore colorful sherwanis and dhotis. The artwork was traditional, and they had a large TV in the corner that always had a Bollywood movie playing in the background. Mrs. Sundaram did all the cooking with the help of another woman, and her husband worked the cash register. It will probably become just another run-of-the-mill BBQ joint."

The incensed look on Nita's face and her silence spoke volumes.

Joyce continued. "Mrs. Sundaram has a daughter up north somewhere, but she told me that she was going to move back to India to live with her brother's family in Calcutta. Her brother was a doctor, and with the health of her husband failing, she thought it best to live their golden years in the house with a doctor."

"Did anybody in the neighborhood say anything to Mr. Happy on their behalf?" Nita questioned Joyce in disbelief, shaking her head and sucking her teeth.

"I don't know if anyone stood up to him on the Sundarams' behalf, but I assure you, we have all had words with Mr. Happy at some point. Everyone in the neighborhood has an ongoing feud with Anthony. That's his real name." A little tongue in cheek, she said, "That's why everyone calls him Mr. Happy—he is anything but *happy.*"

Natalie spoke up. "I thought that was his real name. I call him that all the time."

Her mother shook her head. "His name is really Anthony Grasso. But don't you ever speak to him, Natalie. He is not a nice person," her mother warned her with deep conviction.

"Listen, Nita, I know your husband has Friday night games. We would love to get to know you both better and show you that we are not all a bunch of backwoods racists. Why don't you come over for our bonfire Saturday night after dinner about dusk? You can meet a couple of our neighbors, and we will share all of our Mr. Happy stories. I can't wait to ask Darius what he said to Anthony to make him turn tail like the coward that he really is."

"We would love that. I'll bring the cookies," she said, winking at Natalie.

## CHAPTER 5

# REED AND LEIGH

*Seven days before the killing*
*Reed's side backyard*

"Man, you completely missed the target again," Reed taunted, and Leigh smiled broadly to mask his embarrassment.

He jokingly told Reed, "Screw you."

"That's the second arrow you lost. You'll never find it back past the tree line. How expensive are these arrows anyway?"

"I saw a six-pack from *L.L. Bean* for about thirty-five bucks. I definitely don't want to lose anymore though. Maybe we can look for them later."

Leigh didn't want to disappoint his father after he spent so much money on such a great gift.

"I don't want to spend my own money on arrows. And Dad just bought me a dozen."

"Sure, we can try to look for arrows later, but I'm not promising you anything. You're not going to kill any deer next week if you don't get the hang of this."

"I can look for the arrows for you," Natalie offered, eager to be included and please Leigh and her brother.

"That's okay, sis. Leigh's going to keep practicing. We don't want you to get hurt. If you go into the preserve, Leigh could accidentally shoot you. His aim is not so hot today, or should I say his aim is not on target."

Realizing his wordplay, Reed shot his friend a toying smirk.

"Ha ha, very funny."

Leigh gave Reed a sarcastic side-eye.

Reed started laughing out loud at the stinging remark. "Sorry to be so brutally honest, but I don't want you to shoot my sister, dude."

"You're right. You're harsh, but you're right. I definitely need the practice, and I don't want to hurt sweet Natalie either."

Leigh turned around and faced Natalie with a smile for her kindness.

"Thanks for the offer, Natalie."

She was bubbled with happiness.

Leigh pulled another arrow from the quiver strapped to the bow.

"Thanks, man, for letting me use your yard and woods."

He then placed the arrow on the rest and clipped the arrow onto the string. Natalie stopped collecting her sour oranges and watched the handsome young man in awe as if he were a movie star shooting a film. Leigh pulled back the tight string with his release aid by hooking it on the *D* loop. Leigh lifted his bow and pulled back the string until he reached the mechanical stop on his compound bow, where the tension eased.

"There are too many houses and neighbors and neighbors' dogs to practice in my neighborhood."

He steadied his aim and lined up the front sight with the peep. This time would be different. He carefully looked through the peep sight. The hood blocked the sun so that the conditions were just perfect, and the sun didn't impair Leigh's vision. The magnifying lens in the scope made the burlap target, painted a funky light green, appear closer than it actually was. He zeroed in on the part of the target with the heart painted on the broad side of the deer. Leigh more carefully checked his level this time. No mistakes. Being a bit off level could pull the arrow left or right, like last time, and draw more criticism from his buddy. He kept his position solid with the pin perfectly in the middle. With both eyes open, he pulled a long deep breath, held it a moment, and released.

"Yeah!" Leigh screamed. "That's what I'm talking about!"

He turned to Reed to make sure he didn't miss it.

"Did you see that?"

"Right in the heart!" his buddy exclaimed.

"Let's gooooo!"

Both boys ran up to the imaginary slain buck impaled by the arrow, right behind the front shoulder as intended. Reed clapped his buddy on the back, then put both hands on his shoulders, and leaped into the air as if they were still little boys playing leapfrog. Enjoying the revelry of the boys' celebration, Natalie joined in too.

Running up to the archer, she offered her fist for a fist bump and exclaimed, "Nice shot!"

Reed struggled to free the arrow out from the painted heart of the weathered target with a single hand. He twisted and pulled until it was finally freed. He returned the arrow to Leigh with the flick of the wrist, throwing it directly into the earth next to Leigh's foot and landing upright with the tip of the arrow buried in the sand. Reed congratulated Leigh once more by tussling his friend's curly hair.

"Can I take a turn?" Natalie inserted herself into the male bonding time.

"Not right now, sis. Leigh is trying to hone his skills because he and his dad are going bow hunting in Georgia next week."

"Natalie, I am sorry, but it took me like forty-five minutes or so at Bass Pro Shop to customize the accuracy and to set the resistance perfect for me. Reed isn't even taking a turn. Anyway, I gotta bounce. I still have to write that paper for English Lit, and I have to take next week's biology test early so I can skip school for the Georgia trip. Maybe we can get a couple more practices in later this week before I leave?"

"Sure. In that case, you can leave your stuff in the garage if you want. That way, you don't have to haul it back and forth. Need help?"

"Naw, I got this."

Reed made it up to her. "Sis, you want to go on a golf-cart ride instead? You can drive, and we can go to the point on the far side of the lake."

Everybody was happy again.

Leigh admired how Reed treated his big sister.

"Good, bro."

Leigh pounded his final fist bump and smiled at his friend. Leigh loved his friend without ever having said it.

"Bye-bye, butterfly," Natalie said to Leigh as he collected his belongings.

"See you soon, you big baboon," Leigh returned his part of their salutation to one another.

Reed waved and hollered back to his friend over his shoulder as the siblings drove off in the golf cart.

"Hit the road, horny toad!"

# CHAPTER 6

# DETECTIVE PONTONERO

*7:50 a.m., the morning of the killing*
*Blessed Drive, in front of Anthony Grasso's home*

"Am I permitted to pass? My name is Joyce Kraus, and I live right there?"

With a nod, she indicated to the house next door to the victim.

"I am Detective Pontonero. I need to ask you a few questions."

"May I park at my house first?"

Pont waved her through to the female patrol officer on the street, and she was admitted.

Pontonero walked over to the driveway following Mrs. Kraus as she carefully pulled into the long bricked driveway. While he stood in the driveway, waiting for Mrs. Kraus to shut off her engine and exit her vehicle, Pontonero noticed that it was impossible to see Anthony Grasso's house because of the enormous hedge.

"Do you always park in the driveway instead of the garage?" he inquired.

"Yes, the garage has our golf cart and an ATV and all of my husband's hunting gear."

Her answers were clear and forthright.

"What's happened? Why is there a police car in the street?"

Mrs. Kraus genuinely was surprised and confused as to what was going on.

"Unfortunately, your neighbor was shot." Detective Pontonero paused to phrase it delicately. "And he is no longer with us."

"Anthony is dead?" she responded in utter disbelief, slack jawed. "He was shot?"

The detective waited patiently for the news to settle in.

"Did you notice anything unusual this morning?"

"No."

Her mouth still was agape from the shocking information.

"Do you mind if I come in and look around?"

"Of course not. Please come in. We can go through the garage."

Mrs. Kraus was most helpful, unlike many of the people he had had to investigate over his long career. An occupational hazard developed within Detective Pontonero. He suspected everyone of being a criminal. He believed that every person was guilty of something. They just hadn't been caught yet for their particular crime. So he played the game and pretended to be trusting. Thus, with Mrs. Kraus and other seemingly helpful people, he used his friendly demeanor as a strategy to get intel until which time a different tactic was necessary.

"Where are you coming from?"

"I just dropped my son off at Harmony High School and then got gas from the station on the corner by the school."

"Isn't he a little late? School started at six forty-five."

She turned to the detective with a perplexed look.

"I know because my daughter goes to the same school."

She lifted her chin with better understanding.

"Yes, sir, but he has a biology test during his second period, and I let him skip first period class to get a little more study time in," she responded defensively. "He only missed his yearbook class."

"No judgment passed here, Mrs. Kraus."

He put both hands in the air as if to dismiss the minor school infraction.

"Do you always take him to school?"

"His friend, Leigh Williams, usually takes him, but today, I gave him a ride for extra study time."

They slowly made their way to the garage.

"You mentioned your husband and son. Do you have any other family?"

"Yes, my daughter, Natalie, goes to Harmony High School too."

"Did you give her a ride to school late as well?"

"No, she is a supersenior who has special needs, so they send a bus right to our house. I guess they don't want regular ed students to bully the exceptional ed students, so that is a courtesy they extend to her," Mrs. Kraus explained.

"So I am unfamiliar with the term 'supersenior.' Would you care to elaborate?"

"It just means that she is allowed to stay in school until the age of twenty-two. Instead of doing math and science and regular school subjects, she goes to school to get work training as a custodian, and sometimes in the kitchen as a lunchroom worker, in the hopes of getting hired there, or at a hospital or hotel when she ages out."

Detective Pontonero nodded while the thought percolated.

Once fully in the garage, Pont looked around for the hunting gear Mrs. Kraus mentioned earlier. Fishing rods lined the walls of the garage. Trolling rods hung over layers of other big and bulky saltwater outfits. The heavier outfits masked the freshwater spinners. Right away, he observed the two wooden wardrobes side by side to form a semiwall in the middle of the garage. The camouflaged ATV was parked on one side of the barrier, and the golf cart sat plugged into the electrical outlet bedecked with Christmas lights on the other side. It served as a divider between the single garage door and the double garage door. It could house three cars if it weren't for all the husband's grown man toys. He spied a sticker that formed a duck on the back side of the wooden armoire. If one looked closely, you could see that it was an upside-down fishing hook that formed the head of the duck, and a deer's antler outlined the underside to form the neck and beak.

"So your husband is a fisherman, a duck hunter, and a deer hunter, I take it? Mind if I take a look inside that armoire?"

"Yes, that's right. Please go right ahead. We have nothing to hide. My son hunts and fishes too. Those are just my husband's camo and boots in one wardrobe, and the other wardrobe is for my son's hunting paraphernalia."

Kneeling down low to search the bottom and interior of the wardrobe behind all the hunting apparel, Detective Pontonero uttered, "Well, I don't see the guns or the ammo."

"Come inside. We would never keep them out here to be stolen. I'll show you the gun safe to help your investigation."

Mrs. Kraus ascended the short staircase leading into the house, closely followed by Detective Pontonero. They passed through the kitchen where the morning dishes were still on the table.

"Forgive the mess. I was going to clean up after I got home."

The delicious smell of bacon grease lingered in the air.

"Do you always eat together as a family?" Detective Pontonero asked, checking for an alibi, without asking for an alibi.

"Not usually, but we did today. On most school days, the kids just have cereal on their own, and Ron and I drink coffee on the front porch. But today, I cooked eggs and bacon because of Reed's exam. The gun safe is right over here."

He followed her into a bedroom that was converted into an office. They walked through the den with an open floor plan, passing two mounted deer heads in the living room and one in the study.

"Beautiful mounts."

The detective wanted the woman to feel at ease with him even though he was not a hunter himself and could not understand why anyone would go to that much expense to have dead animals as part of the decor.

"Oh, my husband is extremely proud of those mounts. I told him we could only have one deer head in my home," Mrs. Kraus said, pointing to the original mount in the study. "Then my husband and my son killed those two bucks on the same day. They were so excited. I had to cave in. I told him if he tried to bring another dead creature into my home, his head would be right up there in the middle."

She chuckled at her own joke. She stopped facing the gun safe with both hands on her hips.

"Would you mind opening it?" Detective Pontonero requested, unsatisfied with merely looking at the outside of a closed safe.

"No, not at all. I have to go to the other room to get the key."

As Mrs. Kraus left to retrieve the key to the safe, Detective Pontonero took stock of the three deer and now noticed another beautiful wood duck mounted over the doorframe.

"She should have stuck to her guns," he muttered under his breath, reflecting on yet another life snuffed out unnecessarily.

"Here you go." She handed the detective the peculiar-looking key. "My hands aren't strong enough to get it open. You will have to do the honors yourself. You have to use the same key on the top and then again on the bottom and kind of push in at the same time. It's kind of tricky. I've lost my touch over the years."

The key was circular with a notch located at the side. It was easy enough to line up but difficult to turn and even more so to pull the darn thing out. She was right. He had to lean into the door with his shoulder at the same time as he turned the key. It revealed quite an inventory: one Benelli shotgun, two Mossbergs, a Remington, a Tikka 270, a .243 rifle, a 30-06 deer rifle, a .40 caliber Smith and Wesson handgun, a will, and a small envelope of old pictures. But there was no ammo. If any of the guns had been fired this morning, Pontonero would have smelled it instantly. They were all cold to the touch. The detective took out a small notepad to record the contents of the arms cache.

"Where's the ammunition?"

Just to continue searching the house in its entirety, he continued the ruse of caring where the ammo was kept. In fact, he was looking for any other possible weapon and wanted to enter each and every room of the house until he was convinced the threat did not come from inside this house. She was willingly cooperating without the extra burden of requesting a search warrant.

"Out of an abundance of caution, my husband keeps it hidden in a closet upstairs. He takes safety very seriously."

She no longer appeared at ease. She held her hands in tight fists at her sides and had an uneasy edge about her that wasn't noticeable previously.

"Let's take a little walk and check it out."

Pontonero ducked his head in each room that he passed.

Mrs. Kraus finally had the courage to muster.

"Detective, are we suspects?"

"Do you have reason to kill Anthony Grasso?"

"No. I mean, he was a world-class ass, and everyone I know hated him, but no one hated him enough to kill him, that I know of. Certainly no one in my family."

Alleviating her from her fears, he assuaged her concern with, "Don't worry, Mrs. Kraus, I just want to rule you and your family out as suspects. Now let's take a peek at that closet."

# CHAPTER 7

# NICK AND MINDY MOUNTS

*Two nights before the killing*
*At the bonfire*

"Hey, come on over. Welcome to the neighborhood. You must be the famous Coach Washington we've heard so much about."

Ron greeted the couple, eager to make the new acquaintance. Darius and Nita approached the small gathering, looking like two models from a Peloton advertisement. They both were so fit that they must have been athletes in their high school years. Mr. and Mrs. Kraus stood immediately to greet their new neighbors. They shook hands and patted backs.

"We saw your fire blazing from upstairs, so we thought this was a good time to come over."

Mrs. Kraus greeted her guest. "Absolutely perfect timing. The fire is ablaze, the company is good, and the wine is chilled."

Mr. Kraus made introductions to the couple across the fire.

"I'd like you to meet your neighbors Mindy and Nick Mounts. They live up the street on the corner of Blessed Drive and Peaceful Court."

Nick rose to his feet to extend a firm handshake to the couple, while Mindy remained seated with a bright smile and a welcoming wave, balancing a tray of chocolate bars, marshmallows, and graham crackers on her lap.

"It is a pleasure to meet you. This is my gorgeous wife, Nita."

Darius draped his arm around Nita as she feigned shyness and lightly pinched Darius with a blushing smile.

"And I am Darius Washington."

Ron tweaked his daughter on the cheek. "And this cutie patootie is my daughter, Natalie. She's my little lamb."

"Hello," a muffled salutation came from the happy young lady with sticky marshmallow plastered on the side of her mouth. Her chocolate-covered fingers undulated as she waved with both hands in a friendly gesture.

"I presume you met my wife, Joyce, already?"

"No, actually, my wife did, but this is my first time making her acquaintance. Thanks, by the way, for the brownies, Joyce. The gesture was very kind."

Coach Washington met Joyce Kraus's gaze warmly.

"You are most welcome. Next time, I promise to make you a protein shake," Joyce jested with a smile and a wink.

"I brought chocolate chip cookies as promised." Nita raised the plate, directed mostly at Natalie. "And sliced cheese and fruit for the health nuts like my husband."

Coach raised this bowl with a shrug of his shoulders. "Guilty as charged."

"Please have a seat. Those upright logs are sturdy. You can rest your trays on them and sit on the lawn chairs."

Brightly colored Tommy Bahama beach chairs orbited the fire two feet back, close enough for an intimate chat but far enough away from the fire not to induce a choking spell from the rising smoke.

"Can I get you something to drink, a beer or wine perhaps?" Mr. Kraus politely offered.

"Oh, thanks, man. No, I only drink water. I have to set a good example to my athletes."

"Darius is very health conscious, but I, on the other hand, wouldn't mind one glass of wine."

"Coming right up."

Joyce had already started filling up Nita's plastic red solo cup with a pinot grigio.

Darius acknowledged the quaint names of the streets, eager to fill the awkward silence of people unfamiliar with one another.

"Well, you couldn't have invented a better name for a place to live than that corner, Nick."

"I know," Nick said with a chuckle. "Those names are pretty comical if you ask me. We try to live up to the name. Right, babe?"

Nick gave his wife a little smooch as he eased back into his chair right next to hers.

"I've got to say, living in a town named Harmony and working at a school named Harmony High were part of the appeal of moving here," Coach Washington admitted.

"Joyce was just telling us about your unharmonious encounter with Mr. Happy the other day," Nick added.

Darius shot his wife with a hard side-eye stare. She shrugged back and mouthed "sorry" to him with an apologetic grin.

"Aaah," he sighed. "I really didn't want anyone to hear about that. I don't want to give people the impression that I am a hothead and not in control of my emotions. Especially my athletes and students. Teenagers already struggle with angst and anger management."

"Don't worry about that. You're not the only one to have had a run-in with that guy. We have all had heated encounters with Mr. Happy. That man is so miserable. Who hasn't had a run-in with him is what I want to know."

He looked to the others for support.

Everyone murmured at the same time over one another.

"That's right."

"He's awful."

"What a jerk."

"I hate that guy."

"This is a safe place. What happens at the bonfire stays at the bonfire."

Mindy comforted Darius and tried to put him at ease. Everyone laughed at the tired joke including Darius Washington, albeit less heartily.

Natalie interrupted, "Mom, may I have a cookie?"

"Just one. You already have had a couple of s'mores. You don't want to get a stomachache."

"I am going inside to play video games. I don't want to hear any bad talk about Mr. Happy. Good night, everyone." She looked at her mom. "I got to scat, kitty cat."

Off she headed into the darkness, away from the illumination of the fire.

"Sorry about that. Natalie can't handle hearing a negative word about anyone. Even an evil snake in the grass, like the resident racist next door. That's how we arrived at the moniker 'Mr. Happy.' She doesn't understand the ironic name."

Nita changed the topic slightly. "After the confrontation with him, I have been having the strangest dreams about Mr. Happy."

"They must have been nightmares then," Mindy joked to elevate the mood.

"The night of the confrontation, in the first dream, Anthony is walking across the desert with a snake around his neck dressed in all black. It is nighttime, and it is pitch-black out, and he is just walking toward a bright light, far away over the horizon. The dream was so vivid. When I woke up, I felt like I was there watching him march through the sand. I wasn't walking with him. I was just observing him trudge through the thick sand with great difficulty."

"Have you ever been to a desert?" Nick asked, searching for the possible meaning of the dream.

"No, never, just in books and on television." She looked toward her husband. "I told you about that when I woke up, right, honey?" And he nodded in somber affirmation.

"But I never had the chance to tell you about the second dream. Last night, I had the same exact dream. Only this time, it was daytime, and I could see that a black bird was following him. You know like a crow or raven."

Looking into the eyes around the fire, she held their rapt attention.

"This time, he was still trudging through the harsh desert. He still had a snake draped over his shoulders, but he was walking toward a little white lamb who was standing in a field of flowers. The kind of flowers little kids give to their mom. You know the white ones with yellow centers?"

Cindy offered help. "Daisies, the little white flowers with yellow centers are called daisies."

Nick attempted to lighten the mood, not feeling the rest of the crew's vibe, and was slightly influenced by his alcohol consumption. "No Little Bo Peep to go along with the sheep?"

"No," she furrowed her brow as if still befuddled by the dream. "Then Mr. Happy starts singing and dancing wildly toward the lamb. I woke up feeling so eerie."

"Well, I am not an expert dream interpreter, but I do know that ravens and crows represent death. It is a common symbol in movies and books. Everyone knows that black is not a good color, symbolically speaking. And snakes, for that matter, are bad news too."

Ron laughed inwardly at his own limited knowledge of symbolism and then smiled at his wife to gain her approval. She returned the smile and patted his hand. Ron led the interpretation of the dreams but was quickly picked up by the rest of the group.

Mindy followed Ron's lead right away.

"Let's look it up on the Internet and solve this mystery dream."

Nick sarcastically added, "Okay because we all know how accurate the Internet is."

The entire group laughed at the joke because they all knew that anyone could write or say just about anything on the World Wide Web.

"Just humor me, babe. It's just for entertainment purposes. Do you have something better to do?"

Eager to please his wife and keep the peace, Nick declared, "Okay, I will look up daisies, and you can look up the business of the desert."

Ron Kraus surfed the net on his phone and struck gold first.

"The white light, according to Sensational Color, represents an 'unblemished marker of purity.' White is 'the symbol of truth, unadulterated by dishonesty.' It goes on to say white is 'blinding to people accustomed to the dark' and 'white illuminates the ills of society.'"

"Huh," Ron reflected, "that doesn't really shed light on your dream for me."

"This is what I found," Nick added, his face buried into his phone as well. "According to ftd.com, daisies symbolize innocence and purity. That kind of goes along with what you found, Ron. But it also says that a daisy is really two flowers in one, so it can also symbolize true love."

Still gripping his phone, he dangled the device and looked up at the group.

Nick joked, "Ha! Maybe Mr. Happy is going to get married to lucky lady number four. Perhaps the march through the desert represents the march down the wedding aisle."

"Poor woman. We should probably warn the unfortunate bride," Joyce joined in on the fun. "I'm on the website Ron mentioned. I looked up what the color black signifies. It could mean the lack of love and support. My husband was right." She gave him a quick wink. "Black also represents hate, malice, evil, darkness, and despair. The website says it could represent the juxtaposition of night and day, good and evil, and right and wrong."

Ron responded to his wife. "Maybe that is why this nightmare reoccurred once in the daylight and once at night. Hate and malice are two words that pretty accurately depict Mr. Happy."

Everyone bobbed their heads up and down in agreement to that statement.

"Now we are getting somewhere!" Mindy reported, "My search read that traveling across a desert could be a sign of death!"

Darius stared at his wife in disbelief. While everyone else was entertained at the notion of interpreting Nita's dreams, he was aware that his wife truly believed that dreams had a mystical connection to other worlds. He was well aware that Nita believed dreams were messages sent from beyond. Darius thought his wife probably believed that her father sent her the dreams.

When Nita tried to give her husband a knowing and meaning-ful look, he turned his head to avoid eye contact. He wanted to keep the mood light and not give into her fears.

"Oh my gosh, Mindy, are you on Speakingtree.in?" Joyce asked Mindy excitedly.

Mindy responded, "Yes, I am."

"I thought so. So am I. I read that same thing. Scroll all the way down to what it says about singing and dancing."

Thumbing down her phone, scrolling until she found what Joyce was talking about, wide-eyed, she exclaimed, "Yikes! Too bad for Mr. Happy. Looks like he should plan a funeral right after the wedding."

"Come on, singing and dancing symbolizes death?" Darius asked skeptically. "Psh! That seems more likely to support the idea of Mr. Happy's wedding to me. Nobody that I know sings and dances at a funeral."

"According to this website, it doesn't just represent death," a long pregnant pause later, "but *murder*!"

Mindy exaggerated the word murder for the full effect. Looking around the campfire, she dragged the word out in a deep ghoulish voice until she met the gaze of everyone in the group and giggled at her own hyperbolic drama.

Darius Washington wanted to give the message a more positive spin.

"Ron, to support your theory, I found that snakes could repre-sent fear and threats, a menacing symbol."

In a more encouraging tone, he said more loudly with a slightly raised pitch, "But snakes can also be symbolic of wisdom and peace. We may never understand this dream. It may not be a nightmare at all."

Nita whipped her head around quickly and grabbed her hus-band's wrist.

"No, when I woke up, it definitely left me feeling uncomfort-able." She loosened her grip but continued, "It was very creepy. No, it wasn't just a dream, but a nightmare."

Her shoulders slumped. "It's hard to explain because when I say it out loud, it doesn't sound like a nightmare, but when I woke up, it left me with the effect of a nightmare."

Darius comforted his wife by rubbing her shoulder and placing a strawberry gently in her mouth.

Mindy, now having had two glasses of wine, her maximum for revelry, threw down the gauntlet, looking directly at her husband.

"How would you snuff out Mr. Happy if he is going to be *murdered*, according to the dream?"

Again, her reiteration of the word *murdered* was exaggerated for dramatic effect.

Nick leaped to his feet and acted out the scenario as he unfolded his account.

"I would walk straight up to his door, put a Band-Aid over the peephole, ring the doorbell, and wait patiently for the man to answer. As he opens the door, I would yell to frighten him, 'Aaaaaa!'"

His loud, unexpected scream caught the group off guard and startled everyone around the fire. This stunt elicited the laughter he had intended and fueled Nick's dramatic performance to continue.

"And I would put a katana in his gut and slice him in two like so."

With an imaginary samurai sword in both his hands, Nick thrusted his whole body forward, stabbing the air. One foot actually stepped dangerously close to the fire and then followed through with a jerking, upward motion with the imaginary instrument held high and tightly in both hands, one fist on top of the other.

Everyone applauded Nick for being such a good sport.

"Man, you really show commitment," Darius teased.

Nick's wife articulated, "I was afraid that you were going to tumble into the fire."

"Me too," Joyce blurted to Nick, leaning out of her seat reaching to give Nick a high five to show her approval of his performance.

He took a bow before slowly backing into his seat ever so carefully so that he did not tip the chair over and indeed land in the fire.

"Same here," Nita lipped to her husband about the over-the-top performance.

She appreciated that her husband was a teetotaler. It was difficult to read his mood. She knew he was acting guarded although it was clear to her that the others did not notice. He was probably being judgmental of the "acting while under the influence of alcohol" scene. She would ask him later why he wasn't being his usual talkative self. He wasn't unfriendly, just guarded.

Joyce razzed, "What's up with the Band-Aid?" She looked around the fire to see if the others wondered about the minor point. "An interesting detail, right?"

"That was so he couldn't see me coming, for the element of surprise."

Ron jokingly voiced his concern too. "You better hope Mr. Happy doesn't have a camera on his doorbell like you have, or you would be busted in a minute. Nobody can get away with murder these days. Everywhere you look, there is a camera. Big Brother is always watching. After you have sliced him up, how would you dispose of the body? Would you chop him up and feed him to your guests at the pizzeria?"

"No way. I have a reputation to maintain. I sell the best pizza in Central Florida. Now I might chop him up and feed him to my dogs." A smirk creeped across Nick's face. "That would be a worthy ending for the likes of him."

Nick, by now having a few beers in him, divulged the reason why he would hypothetically kill Mr. Happy and confessed what irritated him the most. His mood changed in actual reflection without the humor of only moments earlier.

"Honestly, I can't stand that man. He is a menace to the neighborhood. He goes around the neighborhood knocking over people's garbage cans whenever anyone puts them out early. Once upon a time, he used to be on the board of our homeowners association and wrote it in as a rule that you were not permitted to take out the trash before 6:00 p.m. the night before garbage day. The problem with that rule is, our garbage men come so early in the morning. You have to put it out the night before. Once people come in from work, they don't go in and set their clocks for six. No, they handle the responsibility when they get home, when they see it in their driveway. Anyway, one evening right before six, I had just put my cans out on the curb. He didn't see me sitting on my front porch when he went in for the kill. I yelled, 'You better not touch my effing garbage cans if you don't want me to break your fingers.'"

"Wow, you actually said that? What did he do?" Nita questioned curiously.

"He kept on walking like the coward he is, looking for other garbage cans to knock down. He just made matters worse. Garbage just gets spread everywhere by the wind and makes all the neighbors mad at each other, when really they should be mad at him."

The mood was getting tense, so Coach Washington added levity by returning to Nick's story.

"Yeah, and when your dogs crap him out, you can pick him up with a doggy pooper scooper and toss his remains in the garbage without fear that someone would kick it over."

Mr. and Mrs. Kraus helped Darius and kicked up the laughter at Coach Washington's joke, but Mindy was now worked up as well.

Mindy chimed in, still angry, "The reason *I* can't stand the man is that he spreads false rumors about my boys. They get into enough trouble on their own without him spreading lies about them."

Hearing the words come out of her mouth, Mindy chuckled at her own embarrassing statement, looking directly at her husband. Nick smirked back and raised his beer in agreement.

"Remember the fire behind our house when the preserve caught fire from sparks across the street?"

This time, the question was addressed to Mrs. Kraus.

"How could I forget? The fire department rolled right through our backyard, plowed over our firepit, and knocked the barbed wire fence down to get to the preserve so they could extinguish the fire," Joyce recounted the story for the benefit of the Washingtons.

Mindy's eyes were now focused on the Washingtons. "Mr. Happy told everybody in the neighborhood that our boys were the ones responsible for starting the fire even though we were the ones that reported the fire. We were all eating breakfast on the back patio when our eldest son noticed the blaze. Nick called 911. Instead of being the heroes, we were made out to be the villains."

"What did you do about it?" Nita inquired.

"Nothing. I am not confrontational like my husband. I just fantasized in my head about killing the man."

"Okay, let's hear it, Mindy. How would you go about murdering Mr. Happy?" Nick asked his wife.

"I thought about slipping him a roofie."

Her husband immediately cracked up.

"Then I would stuff him into one of those small crates he puts his dogs in all day and let him rot away for weeks in his house. No food. No water. It would be years until anyone found the body. Nobody loves him. He has no friends. Who would miss him? His family—or ex-families, I should say—they all hate his guts. He doesn't even have colleagues at work that would notice him gone because he just does road shows selling those motorcycle emblems he patented that he is so proud of. I am telling you *no one* would miss him."

"Baby, where are you going to get roofies? You know those are illegal, right?"

"Well, I am not really going to kill the man, so I don't have to worry about all the minor details. And if I was going to commit murder, do you think I would be worried about buying an illicit drug?"

"I think he means you're a Goody Two-shoes and you would be clueless how to get the drug," Ron jested. "Also, I think the bank might notice when his bills didn't get paid."

Nita picked up where Ron left off. "Everything today is on autopay. Depending on how good his sales were and how big his bank account was padded, that would be the determining factor of when his corpse would be found."

"Point taken, good lady."

Mindy nodded in agreement to her new friend and new neighbor.

# CHAPTER 8

# RON KRAUS

*8:45 a.m., the morning of the killing*
*County engineer's office*

"I am sorry to interrupt your meeting, Mr. Kraus. There is a Detective Pontonero here to see you. He said it is urgent that he speak with you."

"Please send him right away, Brenda." Turning to the surveyors and engineers, he said, "That's enough for this morning. We all have our next steps. Thanks, everyone."

Pontonero waited for the others to file out of the room before he entered.

Ron stood up to greet the detective with a quizzical look on his face.

"Can I help you with something, Detective?"

"Yes, I hope so. Have you spoken to your wife this morning?"

A pit in Ron's stomach developed, and he was overwrought with worry for his family.

"Not since I left her at breakfast. Is there anything wrong at home?"

"Not at your home." Pontonero took a deep breath before delivering the news. "Your neighbor was killed today. Anthony Grasso. Did you notice anything unusual when you left for work today?"

Ron stood numb for a moment. He was relieved instantly that his family was safe but incredulous that his neighbor that he hated for years was no longer on the planet. A new curiosity entered his mind.

"No, nothing out of the ordinary."

Ron took a moment to reflect on his morning.

"I walked the dogs with my daughter early this morning, maybe around five thirty."

Mr. Kraus rubbed his beard while making sure the time was roughly accurate.

"The new neighbor, Coach Washington, was leaving for work as I was getting in my truck around six o'clock. We waved at each other."

Mr. Kraus pointed in the mental direction of his other neighbor's house, using his mind's eye, in relation to his own house.

"Jimmy on the corner is an air traffic controller and works long and odd hours. He is usually gone by 4:00 a.m. So we rarely see him. Today was no exception. Anthony wasn't even home yet when we left for work."

"How do you know that?" the officer interrupted.

"Because he goes to trade shows to hawk his wares and he has that huge motorcycle trailer that takes up the entire driveway when he's home. It has been gone all weekend."

"Is he usually gone on the weekends?" Pontonero continued his investigation.

A bit too surely, he answered, "I don't know, Detective. I don't keep his calendar. I try to avoid that man at all costs. But I do know he goes off a lot of weekends thankfully, so I usually don't have to see him on my days off."

"Why the harsh edge to your words about your dead neighbor?"

The detective was surprised that such a professional man would openly criticize a newly dead neighbor.

Mr. Kraus clicked his tongue in annoyance at the memory.

"Once, several years ago now, I had a screaming match in the street with him because he yelled at my mentally handicapped daughter and my son when they were young. Anthony told my kids he was going to shoot our family dog if it ever got out of the house again."

In an attempt to have the officer take his side, he said, "Kids leave doors open all the time."

Kraus shrugged his shoulders and proceeded. "Man, that set me off."

He leaned in close to the detective and anger rose in the man, remembering the event as if it had just happened yesterday.

"Nobody is going to threaten my family, especially my sweet Natalie, who really worried that she was going to witness the murder of her dog."

Pontonero just stared at the angry man.

Resolutely, Ron continued his thoughts.

"I told him if he ever had a problem with my family to come tell it to my face. I told him in no uncertain terms that he was never to speak to my wife or my kids again, or I would beat him to a bloody pulp."

"And did he ever speak to your wife and kids again?"

"Not for five years since. That coward won't even look at me. My daughter still waves to him because she is so sweet and innocent, and Anthony doesn't even wave back. He knows better."

Remembering that the policeman before him just announced his death, he said, "Well, he knew better."

Changing tact, the detective said, "Your wife tells me you are a hunter. Do you ever bowhunt?"

"No, I never have. My wife already complains that I have too many distractions. She already hates that I am gone so often and plus the expense of another hobby. No way would she allow that. She describes herself as a deer season widow."

"I think I know the answer to this one, but I have to ask. Do you ever take your daughter hunting?"

Ron chuckled to himself, smiled, and relayed a story he was eager to share. His whole demeanor changed. It was evident that he had a special relationship with his beloved daughter.

"Once, when Natalie was in elementary school, she was maybe seven or eight years old, she said that she wanted to go on a dove hunt with me. We both got all suited up in camo and vests. I took her with me to buy the shells at Walmart. I cleaned the shotguns while she watched and danced around the garage, listening to teenybop music. We drove for miles to get to some property that I was invited to hunt with special permission. I even set her up in a foldable camouflage chair. I figured that she could collect the birds for me after I shot them. As soon as I pulled out the gun, she said, 'What are you doing, Daddy?' I said, 'We're going to kill some birds.' She said, 'Oh no, we're not.'"

Earnestly interested, Detective Pontonero asked, "So did you get to hunt that day?"

"No, we did not, nor ever since with her. We spent the remainder of the afternoon at Chuck E Cheese eating cheap pizza and crawling through suspended mazes."

"Thank you for your time, Mr. Kraus. I will let you get back to it."

"Wait, Detective. If I may ask, how did Anthony die?"

"He was shot."

A wide-eyed Kraus responded, "You can talk to Coach Washington. He'll confirm Anthony was still not home when we left for work. Feel free to verify my report time with Brenda too, my administrative assistant, on your way out. She was here when I arrived this morning."

"I will."

"And, sir, if you think I am a suspect, check my records. I don't have any run-ins with the police, I go to church most Sundays, and I used to coach my son's Little League team."

Pontonero chuckled to himself. "None of that precludes you from killing your neighbor. I checked you and your wife out already. I am aware of your wife's public urination / defecation infraction."

Embarrassed, Mr. Kraus looked around to see if anyone overheard the detective through the thin glass-windowed wall. He lowered his voice until it was barely audible.

"She had to pee after a U2 concert, and you know how long the lines are at the women's restroom. She just went between two cars in the parking lot, and boom, it was a sting operation! She didn't even poop. It was just a pee."

The detective smiled at the gentleman as he exited the office, leaving the man standing alone and uneasy.

# CHAPTER 9

# REED KRAUS

*Two nights before the killing*
*At the bonfire*

"Hey, Reed, what brings you out here?" Mrs. Kraus spoke to her son lovingly. "I thought you were going over to play video games with the Mount boys tonight?"

"I am hanging out with them tonight. Sis just said you had s'mores out here, and I thought I would score some before I left."

"Have you met Mr. and Mrs. Washington yet?"

"Nice to meet you, Mrs. Washington." He waved in her direction. "Hey, Coach." He shook the coach's hand.

Coach Washington asked Reed, "Are you in one of my PE classes? You look familiar."

"No, sir, I have Best Buddies PE so I can play unified basketball on my sister's team."

"Wow, that's very noble of you as a little brother."

"No, I'm not being noble. I really love it. I got all my buddies to join in Best Buddies PE too, and we have a blast. It's truly the best part of my day."

Reed noticed that he had the group's rapt attention.

"It's the only time of the day that has absolutely no stress. We're all just friends goofing around. The administration handpicks who's allowed in the class, and there are absolutely no bullies allowed."

Coach Washington nodded his head up and down, familiar with the program and encouraging the teen to carry on.

"If we request it, we usually get in, so it is mostly my sister's class, all of her friends, and all my friends."

Reed broke off a piece of chocolate. He shifted his gaze from Coach to Mrs. Washington briefly and back to Coach.

"Because my friends have all grown up around Natalie, they know how to interact with her, and so they know how to act around other kids with special needs too."

He popped the chocolate in his mouth and let it dissolve.

"So many teenagers are awkward around them and act fake or, I don't know, just treat them differently. I want to rephrase that. So many *people*, even adults like teachers and admin, weird out. This is something I know how to do. I can teach others how to treat my sister kindly without being weird."

An example came to mind.

"We had a basketball game against St. Cloud High School last year. We played in our gym during the school day, and the crowd went nuts every time Natalie scored. I'd get the ball and feed it to my sister, and she kept taking the shot over and over again until she finally sank it. My friend, Jake, he plays football for you, would work the crowd into a frenzy by raising his hands in the air and getting people to get up out of their seats. He would run up and down the court, riling up the crowd, and I swear it was as if the fans were at an Orlando Magic game."

A huge smile overcame Reed at the memory of that game.

"St. Cloud is such a small community, and all the players on both teams grew up playing against each other in Pop Warner and Little League and at the Civic Center. So it really isn't as competitive for us. We even high-five the other team at times and help each other up when we fall."

Coach asked, "So you must be looking forward to this year's game?"

"Yes, sir, we are the away team this year so we get to ride the bus to St. Cloud High School this time, which means we get to skip a couple of classes legally."

Reed said this with a grin while rubbing his hands together. He knew this honest moment would generate a smile or two from his audience.

Nick piped up. "Hey, Reed, which one of you knuckleheads got into my phone and changed your parents and our group message to Old Folks Talking?"

Reed clapped his hands together and laughed hardily. "I'll never tell."

"Yeah, they did it to ours too!" his mother added playfully. "And they added a picture of King Kong to your name, Nick."

Everyone roared with laughter at the newly manipulated profile icon.

Ron encouraged Reed to stick around a little longer by pulling him into the discussion.

"Well, if you have time to chat a bit, son, we were just swapping stories about how we would off Mr. Happy hypothetically."

Reed snickered, "Oh, really?"

Setting the stage to reveal how you would kill someone, especially to a teacher that worked at your school and whom you just met, should be personal and private, yet in front of his parents and his semisurrogate parents, he felt at ease.

"I see we're getting really cozy with our new neighbors right off the bat."

He smiled his handsome smile and jumped right in.

Addressing Mrs. Washington, he said, "Well, you've got to realize, first of all, that he is the *meanest* man on Earth."

"Yes, we had the misfortune of finding that out firsthand," Coach Washington agreed.

Mrs. Kraus explained to her son and the others, "Mr. Happy called the Washingtons the N-word."

"No way!" A long pause hung in the air. "That is messed up." Reed followed it up with, "But I'm not surprised at all. That man used to break glass bottles and hide them in the thick St. Augustine grass where you couldn't see them to pop our tires and keep us from riding our bikes in his grass."

He turned to his mother. "You remember my friend Ty, who used to live in our neighborhood?"

She nodded that she did.

"He fell once on his broken bottles and sliced his hand something fierce. He was hurt so bad. He had to go to the hospital for stitches. Ty's mom called the cops, but nothing happened to Mr. Happy. They just made him pick up the glass and told him not to do it again, or they would bring him to jail for reckless endangerment."

Sarcastically, Reed added, "I guess you can only go around hurting kids on purpose like that just the one time and get away with it."

"Okay, so how would you kill Mr. Happy, son?" his dad reiterated the question.

"That's easy. We already joked about it this summer when we went fishing in the Keys with my mom and dad for my birthday."

Looking at the adults around the firepit, he said, "It was a beautiful day. We were laughing and cracking jokes. Everybody was in a great mood because we caught mahi earlier in the morning. We were offshore twenty-three miles out when all of a sudden, the weather changed, and the sky darkened black, and the waves were cracking over the gunnels. The mood instantly changed. No one was speaking. My heart was pounding."

He looked at his dad, who winced in return.

"I took in all the rods. Dad was trying his best to keep the bow of the boat heading into the waves so we didn't capsize. Both my mom and dad looked terrified. And mom finally yelled over the wind what we were all thinking. 'A man could easily lose his life out here!'"

Mr. Kraus added, "Each of us confessed we were all praying to make it back to the shore alive that day."

His mother exhaled sharply as she vividly recalled that excursion.

Reed pressed on. "So how would I kill Mr. Happy? I would take him fishing on a day when the seas were rough and help him out of the boat."

# CHAPTER 10

# RON KRAUS

*Two nights before the killing*
*At the bonfire*

"Dad, I am curious. How did you kill Mr. Happy?"

"I haven't taken my turn, son."

Ron squeezed the empty can and tossed it into the fire. His eyes transfixed on the paint melting off the can.

"You actually stole my idea. I was going to throw him overboard out at sea too. It would be so easy to get away with it if you were any good at acting. But if anyone knew Anthony, they'd immediately suspect foul play because who would willingly invite him on a day out on the boat?"

This remark elicited a chuckle from the group.

"I'm sure you can come up with another way to kill him off," Nick encouraged the banter to continue while he helped himself to a second beer.

"Okay, I thought of something. The next time he comes banging on my door and opens up his stupid trap about my dogs getting out and how they should be kept in a crate when I'm not at home, I'd catch him off guard and yank him into the house."

Ron looked around at all the smiling faces staring back at him.

"Then I would beat him to a bloody pulp like I always wanted to. Next, I'd tie him up in the garage and wrap that old painter's tarp around him."

He looked at Nick and pulled a funny face.

"I've been meaning to clean up the garage."

Nick tossed his head back with a smile at the joke.

"Then I would tie Mr. Happy to the ATV and drag him out back around for a while in the preserve. We'd ride over every fallen log, every muddy hole. I'd take him off the beaten path through all the brambles. When that stops being fun, I would drop him off in the swampy area and let the wild hogs have their fun with him. They are filthy, disgusting creatures just like him."

He looked at his new neighbor Nita. "They would eat a man."

Nita responded by making a disgusted face and shuttered at the thought of it.

"Whatever was left of him, the gators would devour."

"That's just nasty," Joyce piped up.

"Well, my lovely bride, how would you go about killing Mr. Happy then?"

"Oh no. Not me. I believe in karma. No schadenfreude for me."

Mrs. Mounts gave her friend a quizzical look. "Schadenfreude?"

"That's when you get enjoyment from someone else's pain and turmoil," Mr. Kraus explained, helping his wife out.

"If I wish a terrible fate to befall that terrible man, his terrible fate could rub off on me. No thanks. Believe me, something awful *will* happen to that man because what goes around comes around. I do not need anything to come around to me. Plus God knows my heart. I'm trying to get to heaven." She pointed to the heavens.

"You are so sweet, dear. Natalie must come from your side of the family, while Reed has a bit of his daddy in him. You saw how fast he joined the fun, right?"

"He's a chip off the ole block," Mrs. Mounts added, licking the sticky off each finger, one at a time.

"Reed, you could take the meat to work and feed it to the gators."

"No thanks, I don't want the gators I feed at work to start enjoying the taste of man. They might see me as dessert. On that note, I am off to kill some Nazis."

Reed bid adieu and headed off into the darkness with extra s'mores in hand for the road.

# CHAPTER 11

# AMANDA GRASSO

*8:50 a.m., the morning of the killing*
*Mrs. Grasso's apartment*

"Can I help you?" Amanda opened the door slightly to hide the fact that she was just dressed only in her pajamas.

"Sorry to wake you, ma'am. I am Detective Hannon with the St. Cloud Police Department. Are you Amanda Grasso?"

"I am Amanda Grasso, but you didn't wake me. I was just heading to bed. I just got home from my graveyard shift at the hospital. What's all this about, Detective?"

"I am sorry to inform you, but your husband, Anthony Grasso, is dead. He was killed sometime this morning around dawn or just before."

"WHAT? You are kidding?"

Her facial expression was difficult to read. Hannon couldn't make out if it was excitement or shock that the woman displayed.

"They finally did it," she muttered under her breath.

Mrs. Grasso stared blankly past the detective for a moment.

"I'm sorry. What's that?" He missed whatever it was she mumbled.

She spoke up. "Soon to be an ex-husband. I've filed for a divorce."

Whatever was her first reaction, her second reaction, she appeared comforted.

"If you don't mind me saying so, you don't seem too upset by the news."

"I am actually relieved," Mrs. Grasso explained. "He won't be bothering us anymore." She hung her head and momentarily closed her eyes. "The man was a tyrant. Even after we moved out, he would stalk us and threaten us and try to control who we could and couldn't see. I even have a restraining order against him."

"Yes, I looked into that before I knocked on your door."

"Do you know who did it?"

"That is what we are looking into now, ma'am. May I ask why you were seeking a divorce?"

"Anthony was a bully. He was constantly riding my son and me. I could take it, but my son is fifteen, and you know how teen boys can be."

"Not really. How can they be?"

Detective Hannon was trying to lure Mrs. Grasso into incriminating herself or her own son.

"Well, Anthony has always been physical with me. A slap here, a push there. Then one day, Anthony pushed me down the steps. I wasn't hurt too bad. It was just a few stairs, but it was the thing that put Charlie over the edge."

The detective's face looked pained by this.

"Charlie thought he was old enough to take Anthony on, which he clearly was not, so Charlie bowed up to him. One punch and Charlie laid in a puddle of blood, lying on his back. My son was actually knocked out for a second or two. That was the one time Anthony knew that he had gone too far. He didn't even follow us out the door like he usually did. Normally, he would drag us back inside, not so that we weren't on full display for the neighbors to see us but to control us, you know?"

She paused for a moment, reliving the unpleasant memory in her head.

"I picked Charlie up, and we left that godforsaken house, and we never looked back. We came straight to this apartment, and we could not be happier. Charlie is making new friends in this neighborhood, and his grades are getting better too. Truth be told, we should have left much sooner."

"If he was so controlling, why did he just let you leave?"

"I told him I would kill him if he ever touched my Charlie ever again. He knew I meant it too. One night, in a previous fight, I confessed to him that I had a plan to kill him by stealing drugs from the hospital, and no one would ever be the wiser. And he knew I could do it too."

"You never reported him to the police?"

"No, so as far as you knew, we were a happily married couple until I got the restraining order."

"So you threatened his life?"

"Yes, but I was not the only one. He was always in a beef with everyone. For example, Anthony fought with the fire department while they were trying to save our neighbors' lives and their property. He was angry and started yelling at them and trying to prevent them from doing their job because they knocked down our back fence to create a firebreak so that the fire didn't take out the houses along the backside of the preserve and maybe all of our houses, during the Harmony Preserve fire a couple of years ago."

The detective interjected, "Sometimes, the fire department has to do a little damage to prevent it from getting worse."

"One of the firemen said they should let the fire take our house with him in it before putting out the flames."

A new example came to mind. "Another time he fought with the garbage men because Anthony kept putting cans of stain and paint in the garbage cans and they refused to take it, along with the palmetto stumps that he cut too big."

"Yes, toxins have to be taken to the dump so that they dispose of the contamination properly."

"Well, they wrote him nasty grams and stuck them on the garbage cans. They refused to take them unless he cut the palmetto stumps into smaller pieces and deposited the toxins at the dump."

"So what would Anthony do?" the detective asked.

"He flew off the handle and called them terrible names, and he told them to go back to Africa."

"Wow," Detective Hannon uttered in disbelief.

"Can you believe that?"

He shook his head in response.

"One of the garbage men ran over to beat up Anthony, but he ran inside before he could get to him. The garbage man chased right after him all the way to the front door and tried to come through it, but Anthony had locked it just in time. Then the man yelled at the top of his lungs, through the door, that he was going to 'get' him."

She shook her head at the recollection.

"After the man left, Anthony acted like nothing even happened."

Imagining the house across the street, in her mind, she pointed to nothing in particular.

"I had to drag my cans to the neighbor's house after that because they would drive right past our house after that little incident. He was always getting threats because he was such a hater and troublemaker."

She continued with examples of stories of his enemies because the detective was such a good listener.

"The neighborhood kids used to put piles of dog dirt on our porch all the time to get back at him for how terrible he was to children."

He laughed inwardly at her euphemism for dog crap.

"If they rode on the sidewalk, while they were riding their bikes, he would squirt them with the garden hose. Not in a fun playful way but a cruel way, cussing and taunting them for his own pleasure. He actually kept stones in his pockets sometimes so he could throw rocks at people, at *children*, and at dogs."

She drew her hands to her temple.

"Charlie was humiliated by this and begged him not to mess with the kids in the neighborhood, but Anthony could care less. He took pleasure in hurting people and animals too, for that matter." She shrugged. "There is no other way to say it. He was just sadistic."

Hannon knew this was an incendiary question and asked it anyway.

"If he was so awful, why would you marry such a man?"

"Because, Detective," she said with a great sigh, thoroughly desolated by the question and memory of her time with her husband, "he tricked me. He never reared his ugly head until after we married. You have to understand, I was a single mother of Charlie. I had no other prospects at the time, and I wanted Charlie to grow up with a father figure. He seemed like a good provider, and he was easy on the eye. We met and were married within three months, just short enough time for him to hide the monster that he really was."

"Do you have any prospects now?"

"Do you mean am I dating anyone now? No, Detective, I have no boyfriend. Anthony would never allow that. Even separated."

Detective Hannon stared at Amanda Grasso but was not unsympathetic to her situation. He had witnessed women like this his entire career, trapped in a loveless marriage with no emotional support outside of the marriage, and most often, they would stick around longer than prudent because a child was involved.

"Detective, I can see the wheels spinning in your head. Was Anthony killed from an injection? A drug overdose?"

"That is for the forensic team to determine, but for now, it does not look that way."

A seed firmly planted in his mind—note to self, check the autopsy for poison or chemicals.

"I am a nurse, Detective. It is my job to heal people. I said it out of fear and frustration because I felt trapped, and the threat seemed like my only way out. The threat seemed like it leveled the playing field. For a while, it worked. I never meant it. I will give you my head nurse's phone number so you can verify with her that I was working all night. I can text it to you."

"No, just write her name and number here, please, on this pad. I like doing it the old-fashioned way."

"I called my son to wake him and once more forty-five minutes later to make sure that he was getting to the bus stop to go to school. Before you accuse Charlie of anything, call his school, Osceola High School. Charlie has Anthony's last name, Grasso, so that we could all have the same last name, as a family. They can prove that he was on the bus and in class on time, right where he should be."

She handed the pad back to Detective Hannon.

"Did Anthony pay child support?"

She answered sarcastically, "Ha ha, yeah right. That never happened."

"Well, on the bright side, you might inherit his money, his business, and his house now that he is dead, and you are not officially divorced."

She looked concerned suddenly at the implication.

"If you think of anything helpful, here is my number."

She unfolded her arms to receive the card.

"Get some rest, Mrs. Grasso. I'll keep in touch."

# CHAPTER 12

# NITA WASHINGTON

*Two nights before the killing*
*At the bonfire*

"So, Nick, why did you choose to kill Mr. Happy with a samurai sword? It seems a little bit of a stretch to have one of those just lying about."

Just the invitation Nick was waiting for to discuss his collection of interesting blades from around the world.

Nick perked up, and his once relaxed shoulders leaned forward with enthusiasm as he regaled in his collection of knives.

"We have been going to trade shows ever since our first pizza franchise when we were struggling to make ends meet. We mostly just looked around then. I would buy the occasional pocketknife when I could afford it. My first purchase was this sweet little Swiss Army knife. This gem has twenty-six different functions."

"It's amazing how many tools are hidden in those things," Mindy added to support her husband's excitement.

"See this one here."

Reaching into his pocket, Nick pulled out a fat, red pocketknife and extended out each of the tools until he placed a bone-colored piece of plastic into his mouth to suck on.

"It even has a little toothpick."

Mindy proudly shared. "With every new store we acquired, we celebrated by buying another blade from around the world or an epoch piece from the United States."

"How many blades are you up to?" Darius asked while popping a grape in his mouth.

"Twenty-two *unique* blades since the purchase of our latest restaurant on International Drive. We have twenty-two stores in total. Of course, I do have other knives in the collection that I don't include in the count. I want to get a magnetic holder like they have in the movie *Knives Out* so they can be displayed in a circle behind the head of the table. Quite a dramatic effect when you sit down to eat, don't you think?"

"That would look pretty cool. It would have the dramatic effect of a throne. Like the Iron Throne in *Game of Thrones*!" Nita declared.

"Call him King Nick," Mindy flirted with her husband with a wink and a brush of her hand on her husband's knee.

Nick adjusted the imaginary crown on top of his head and continued talking about one of his favorite topics.

"We even have a bayonet from the American Revolution. It is quite the conversation piece. It looks like a metal tube with an elbow bend and then a sword about a foot and a half long. You should come over to the house and see it sometime. We have it displayed in the living room."

"We'd love that." Mrs. Washington smiled at Darius and answered for both of them.

"So we have Mr. Happy thrown overboard by our favorite seafarer, Reed. Our nature lover, Ron," Nick unfolded his hand and motioned toward Ron, "has Mother Nature completing the circle of life. And I have to say, now I am a bit worried about eating any brownies my wife bakes for me the next time she gets mad at me."

Everybody chuckled.

"I have to agree with the resident pacifist," nodding toward Joyce. "I, too, believe in karma. But it's his karma that I would be facilitating."

Everybody laughed at this also, with the exception of Darius. Darius stared at his wife in disbelief.

"All the good methods have been spoken for, so I guess I would run him over with my car."

"Babe?" Darius shook his head and looked at his wife, slack-jawed, as if to say, "What are you saying?"

"What? I wouldn't want to get my hands dirty." She playfully got into the act.

An exaggerated sigh burst out of Darius. "That's not what I mean."

"Honey," Nita explained to her husband, "it's just pretend. No one is serious here. Right?"

She looked around the fire for support. Everyone was quick to respond, bobbing heads up and down, yessing.

"We're just joking," Nick protested.

"Yes, really, Darius, we're just blowing off steam. No one here has a real vendetta against Anthony."

"You are absolutely right, I know. I get it. I was just a little taken back by Nita's joining in on the fun. It is not usually like her to talk about violence so freely."

"Okay. For you, dear, I will hang up the car keys."

Nita snapped her fingers.

"How about death by chocolate? No, wait. I could tickle him to death."

Darius swatted her hand away with a sour puss before she landed a good tickle.

## CHAPTER 13

# DARIUS WASHINGTON

*11:20 a.m., the morning of the killing*
*Harmony High School*

"Johnson, when you are deadlifting, keep that bar close to your shins."

Coach Washington floated around the circuits, looking to fix any lifts that need adjusting to keep his students healthy and strong.

"Jameson, keep your eyes up when you are doing your back squats. Do you see the line where the ceiling and the wall meet?"

"Yes, sir."

"Keep your eyes fixed there, and don't curve your back so much. Use your powerful legs."

"Thanks, Coach."

"The same thing goes for your front squats as well."

The phone rang in the weight room. A maze of circuit training weights and athletes blocked Coach Washington from the phone.

"Want me to get that for you, Coach?" a helpful student resting in between circuits yelled from across the room.

"Yes, please. Thanks."

He hollered from across the room, "The office wants to know if you want a teacher's assistant to escort a detective to the weight room or if you want them to get someone to cover your class for you?"

"Is it an emergency?"

"She said it is not an emergency, but the detective said it is urgent," he hollered once more.

"Send him down with a TA, please.

"TJ, quit texting and put your phone away. You're his spotter, and he is counting on you. That kid is bench-pressing two hundred pounds, and he could crush his windpipe while you are trying to flirt with some pretty young girl sitting in algebra. She's probably getting in trouble from her teacher right now because of you," Coach teased his student after the reprimand to win him back over and build rapport.

"No, Coach, it's not like that. I was texting my mom."

"Okay, well, after class, you can ask what's for dinner. Right now, your job is trying not to kill your partner. Jameson, take a break. Keep an eye on all the spotters, and just make sure nobody else is texting their mom about dinner plans. I'll be right outside this door if you need me for anything. I mean it, James. Keep your eyes peeled."

Coach stepped out the door, curious about what a detective would need to speak to him about. Surely, his mess in Atlanta didn't follow him here.

The TA saw Coach Washington in the hall outside of the gym and weight room waiting for the visitor. The TA pointed to the coach and allowed the detective to walk unescorted the remainder of the corridor by himself.

"Detective Pontonero," the detective said, handing Washington his card. "Do you mind if we talk out here in the hall for privacy?"

"That's fine. The guys are just doing their circuits. They don't need me to babysit. What is so urgent that you need to see me at school while students are still here? Is my wife okay?"

"Yes, as a matter of fact, we spoke to your wife this morning. She's fine." He shrugged his shoulders. "Maybe a little shaken after finding Mr. Grasso, your neighbor across the street, shot dead in the driveway."

There was a shocked look on Washington's face, and he was shaking his head back and forth in disbelief.

"It was all hypothetical. It was just a game. Please tell me that they didn't follow through with it?"

"What was hypothetical? Who didn't follow through with it?"

Detective Pontonero was surprised by Washington's remarks and completely caught off guard. He thought this was going to be a routine questioning and truthfully wasn't expecting to glean much information from the conversation.

"My wife and I were invited to meet the new neighbors. The other neighbors across the street that lived next to Mr. Happy, catty-corner from my house, had a party." With the tilt of his head, Darius reconsidered his word choice, "Not so much a party, as a bonfire."

"Mr. Happy?" Pontonero wasn't following.

"That is what everybody called Anthony Grasso."

"Who is everybody?"

"The Kraus family was there. Joyce, Ron, Natalie for a bit, and then later the son for a little while. I forgot his name. I am really bad at remembering names. That is one of the hazards of teaching and coaching. You learn a hundred new names, and the next semester or at least by the following year, you get a whole new batch."

"Reed. I just checked with the front office about his attendance and his sister's too."

"Yes, Reed, that's right. And I met Mindy and Nick Mounts as well."

Lost in thought, he shook his head as if to clear his mind.

"Anyway, they were all joking about how they would kill Mr. Happy. Mindy started it, asking how people would kill the dude."

Pontonero pulled out a small notebook and started jotting down notes.

"How did each person hypothetically kill off the victim?"

"When you phrase it like that, it sounds bad."

"Yes. It is quite serious. The methods of killing from the night of the bonfire, please," Pontonero pressed again.

Shifting his stance and rubbing the back of his neck to self-sooth, Darius tried to recall who said what.

"Well, the neighbor down the street, Nick Mounts, sliced him in two with some old Japanese sword. His wife drugged him and then starved him to death, I guess, in a dog crate."

Realizing how bad it sounded, he put both hands on top of his head and took a moment to breath. He summoned the courage to continue.

"The boy across the street—"

"Reed," Pontonero supplied the name.

"Yes, Reed, he threw Anthony into the ocean, so I guess he drowned or was eaten by sharks maybe. The father, Mr. Kraus, tied him to his ATV and dragged him around the preserve and left him for the hogs and gators to eat in the swamp."

"What did Mrs. Kraus have to say?"

"She didn't want to participate. She said something about schadenfreude and wanting to get to heaven, so… I guess she was the smart one of the bunch."

"What does *schadenfreude* mean? Sounds German," the detective asked.

"Yeah, probably is German. It's when someone gets happy because someone else is miserable."

"Did your wife kill him off at the bonfire? You didn't mention her story."

Darius exhaled loudly and blurted out, "She ran him over in her electric car."

Pontonero actually laughed at that one, putting Darius slightly more at ease.

"And you? You didn't hypothetically murder Mr. Grasso?"

"No," he said emphatically. Then he added, "Thank God."

"I thought you just moved in. Why would they trust you enough on a little secret of murder if they didn't know you?"

"You're right. They wouldn't if they were serious."

He wiped his face with relief and threw both hands on his hips in a wide stance, typical of coaches who stood on their feet all day.

"It couldn't be any of them. We were all just joking."

Detective Pontonero pushed Washington further.

"But why would you even joke about something like that with someone you had just met?"

"They were just trying to make me feel better."

Pontonero just stared at the man, not letting him off the hook until he continued.

"I had a run-in with the guy earlier this week."

"What happened earlier in the week?" Pontonero prodded because Darius was churning it over in his mind, and he was reluctant to speak.

The longer Pontonero glared, the more uncomfortable Washington became, and finally, he broke his silence. They always do.

"Oh, he just called us some pedestrian, racist terms. The cracker is so stupid. He didn't even land a painful dart at my wife. His words may have had more of an impact if he had used the correct slur for her race. She is Indian. Anthony threatened that he wanted to 'do some coon hunting this weekend.'"

"Whoa…those are some fightin' words. How did you respond?"

"I didn't tell the neighbors, and I didn't even tell my wife, but I will tell you because I want you to believe me when I tell you that we had nothing to do with it."

He stared into Detective Pontonero's eyes fixedly for a long gaze, determining if he could trust this man or not with his future.

"When he threatened me and my wife to go coon hunting, I stood nose to nose with him to let him know that I was serious and told him 'White men aren't the only ones who carry guns.'"

Nodding, Detective Pontonero took a deep reflective breath.

"I respect your honesty, Coach Washington. Did you notice anything when you left for work?"

"No, I didn't even see Mr. Grasso. I thought he was gone all weekend. It was still dark when I left my wife at breakfast. The only person I saw was Mr. Kraus. He was heading off to work in a tie and coat. He waved at me, and, of course, I waved back, and he followed me out to the highway when we each went our separate ways."

"You told Mr. Grasso White people weren't the only ones who carried. Do you own a gun, Mr. Washington?"

"Yes, and before you ask, I have a concealed permit to carry. It was the very first thing I unpacked after I set up our bed, and you will find it remains still under my mattress, unfired, with six bullets still in the cylinder."

"Just curious, Mr. Washington. Why didn't your wife mention the bonfire and all the threats made on Anthony Grasso this weekend?"

"You would have to ask her, Detective. You yourself told me that she was shaken up."

"Another thing, Mr. Washington…"

"Please, people call me Coach. Mr. Washington is my father."

"All right, Coach, before I set foot in your gym, I ran your name for outstanding warrants."

Terrified and defensive, Coach Washington interrupted, "I don't have any outstanding warrants."

"No, Coach, you don't have any outstanding warrants, but you do have a jacket. You want to tell me how a nice guy like you has an assault and battery charge in Atlanta?"

Darius Washington softened his voice and his manner. "Please don't let this get out." He begged in a hushed tone, like his life depended upon it, "Please, I could lose my job."

"I am not making you any promises. Talk."

"It was a Black Lives Matter protest. We were being peaceful, and agitators were screaming at us and spewing rotten things. Everything just got out of hand, and this one guy just wouldn't get out of my face. It was not my finest moment. We were both arrested. I've learned from my mistakes."

"It seems like you have quite a temper, Coach. It sounds like you have a short fuse when it comes to racial tension."

"Just check my gun. Don't you have a way to know if a gun has been fired, like gunpowder residue or something? Also, contact Ron Kraus. He will corroborate that we left the house at the same time, and Anthony wasn't even home yet. I signed in early for a quick workout before the students arrived. At this school, we punch a time clock. Not to get paid hourly, just to know who has reported to school and who needs a class covered in the event of a teacher 'no call, no show.' I will walk you over to the wall so you can see for yourself."

"That won't be necessary. You could have had a fellow teacher punch you in."

"But the schools have cameras. It will prove that I'm not lying. I'm innocent, but I could still lose my job if they find out about what went down in Atlanta. I'll take off work and show you."

"You will do no such thing. I have to insist. You will stay here all through the school day and go to football practice and act like nothing's wrong. Let me do my job. I don't want to see you lose your job."

Pontonero eased off a bit. "You need to concentrate on leading these boys to victory. And I need to figure out what happened to your neighbor. I won't need to bring up your criminal history because the county is already aware of it. They run thorough background checks on all their employees, and believe me, there will be no more second chances if there is another violent run-in, I would imagine. I suspect you would not have a job in the first place if you weren't a top-notch coach, with an unbelievable winning record."

With that, Detective Pontonero spun on his heels and, facing away from the stunned and bewildered coach, threw his hand in the air with his fist in a ball, pinky and thumbs out in the longhorn tradition.

"Aloha."

# CHAPTER 14

# DETECTIVES PONTONERO AND HANNON

*12:10 p.m., afternoon of the killing*
*Meat and Fire*

"Hey, Pont, I ordered you a slab of ribs, okra, and sweet potato casserole."

Don nudged the tray in Pontonero's direction. The ribs were slathered in Sweet Baby Ray's barbecue sauce that spilled over onto the plate and were still freshly steaming.

"I see you had the usual," Pont said, pointing at the half-eaten pork sandwich and baked potato with just the empty skin remaining on the plate while the barbecued baked beans so far remained untouched.

"Sorry, I started without you because I thought you might have been caught up at the high school, and I still have a lot to do this afternoon."

"Actually, you're right. I still want to talk to the Kraus kids before school ends today. I'll have to make this a quick lunch. I need to get back to Harmony High School before dismissal. The daughter is working the lunch rush in the back of the cafeteria, so I decided I would just come back after we had a chance to *ketchup*," Pont said, lifting the condiment in the air to drive home the joke.

"Ha ha ha, you are so punny today. Okay, so let's catch up. Where has the investigation led you this morning?"

"Get a load of this. This past weekend, there was a bonfire at the neighbor's house in which Mr. Happy's demise was discussed."

"Was the murder possibly planned?"

The detective squished his face in a distorted manner and cocked his head to the right.

"That would make it first-degree murder if there was indeed forethought of the homicide," Pontonero shared his newly found information with his partner right away and popped a couple of pieces of fried okra into his mouth.

Confused, Hannon asked, "Mr. Happy?"

"Yes, according to Coach Washington, that's what the neighborhood called our vic."

They both broke out laughing simultaneously.

"Our victim was apparently quite the charmer."

The sarcasm dripped like the sauce off his ribs.

"Anything credible from the threats?" Hannon asked while gobbling down the last of his sandwich.

"Well, it did give me two more leads to investigate. A Mr. and Mrs. Mounts, neighbors down the street and both attendants of the bonfire. I found out that Coach Washington, the new neighbor, was met by the welcome wagon with the threat of gun violence and your basic run-of-the-mill-hate speech by the recently departed."

"Let me guess. He, being a teacher and levelheaded, walked away from the threat of gun violence and went inside immediately and called the threat into our fraternal brethren?"

"That is a swing and a miss, Detective Hannon. No, his philosophy was more in line with fight fire with fire. He told the 'cracker' that 'Black men owned guns too.'"

He raised his first two greasy fingers of each hand in air quotes.

"I was also surprised to learn that Mrs. Washington was Indian." Pontonero paused for a moment to expose his vulnerability. "Does that make me a racist?"

"What did you think she was?"

"With a last name like Washington, I guess I thought she was biracial maybe or just a light-skinned Black woman. Gorgeous either way. I would like to date someone like her."

"Pfft," Don Hannon scoffed. "First of all, that is her married name, and *B*, in your dreams, old man."

"You are older than me."

"Yeah, but I'm not the one making googly eyes at a potential suspect, half his age either."

"I am not making googly eyes at anyone. And she is not half my age either. I am just observing that she is an attractive, helpful, potential suspect, potential witness, reporter of the recently deceased."

"Oh, brother...why would that make you a racist anyway? I think you are a racist if you make broad negative thoughts about an entire group of people based on specifics that may or may not apply. Just because you are not any good at identifying people from different heritages, well, I don't think that qualifies you as a racist."

"With the political climate the way it is now, I want to stand on the right side of history and act appropriately."

"You are politically correct for an old-timer. Maybe just don't look for someone to date at work, especially in our line of work."

He laughed, causing his shoulders to move up and down, but no sound actually accompanied the movement.

"Now what about the neighbor who crossed the crime scene this morning? What did you learn about her?" Hannon asked, lowering his sandwich. "Or did her beauty blind you too?"

"Mrs. Kraus, a perfectly fine-looking woman herself," tongue in cheek, "was quite helpful. She allowed me complete access to the entire house. She never asked for a warrant and hadn't even time to clean up the morning dishes."

He paused to sip his sweet tea.

"The son and husband are proud duck and deer hunters. I took a detailed inventory of the extensive cache of guns they own. Mr. Kraus uses safety precautions with their weapons. The guns are clean and unloaded in a gun safe, and the key is kept separately in a different room. The wife had trouble opening the safe, so she would not be able to transfer guns in and out alone. They have alibis for each other. They all ate breakfast together, according to Mrs. Kraus."

Pont took a moment to wipe off excess sauce from his fingertips.

"I will corroborate this with the kids when I see them this afternoon. Mom kept the boy home from school to study for a test. She checked him in second period. The high school attendance officer verified the daughter rode the special needs bus to school as usual. The family may have driven right past the corpse and didn't even notice him."

Pontonero tasted the sweet potato before he continued.

"I paid a visit to Mr. Kraus as well. According to both Mr. Kraus and Coach Washington, the victim had not come home from the trade show until after both men had both gone to work just before dawn. It was still dark out when they left for work, but there is a streetlamp at the end of the driveway, and by both accounts, they waved at one another."

Pontonero finally finished apprising Detective Hannon what he had gleaned from the morning investigation.

"Go ahead and finish your lunch. I'll catch you up to speed with my industrious morning. I found absolutely nothing at the house. Apparently, whoever caught Anthony Grasso off guard did so before he ever made it inside the house. The truck was still running, as you mentioned this morning, and all the doors to the house were still locked. The garage doors were both closed, no stray bullets found, no bullet holes, no casings. I sent the truck to the lab to be dusted for the usual things, fingerprints, hair, and trace evidence. I even asked the boys to put it on a lift to see if there was anything we missed underneath the vehicle.

"Have you heard back from them yet?" Pont asked, a mouth muffled with smoked pork.

"Nah, too soon. I'll give them a little time to do their work. I did, however, have an interesting dialogue with Mrs. Grasso."

"What did the blissfully wedded Mrs. Grasso have to say? 'Look no further. I am your culprit, and you can move on to your next case now'? I am guessing that he was as good a husband as he was a neighbor and citizen?"

"Even worse, he beat up the kid, Charlie. Consequently, the wife and stepson fled to a new apartment. She filed for divorce and—drumroll, please."

Fingers thrummed from the other side of the table.

"She threatened to kill him with stolen drugs from the hospital."

Pont swallowed and nodded his head with understanding and asked, "Do you like her for this?"

"Well, maybe if forensics comes back with the tox screen that says there is something unnatural in his system. But I don't see her as a shooter especially now that they were finally away from him after being terrorized for so long. She seemed content to me to just be away from the situation."

He picked at the meat lodged in his teeth with a wooden toothpick.

"Mrs. Grasso says she has an alibi. I still have to verify that with her hospital administrator. She claimed that she worked all night and called to wake her son, Charlie. He rode the bus to school, and I called the school to verify his attendance. They only have one car, and he doesn't drive yet. She was heading to sleep when I got there this morning. They moved to Kissimmee. I did a GPS search on Google Maps from the hospital to his house, and it is a thirty-four-minute drive one way to Anthony's house."

Hannon briefly showed his phone to Pont with the two screen-shots of the search before continuing.

"It's a thirty-eight-minute drive from her house to his. There is no way she or the son could have killed the husband and got back to her apartment in that timeline, if she is indeed telling the truth. After lunch, I will head over to the hospital and see what I learn about Mrs. Grasso and verify her version of the truth."

"Okay. So that's good. We are ruling out our suspects. I need to get back to the high school so that I can talk to the Kraus kids before they get home and talk to one another. Can you check out Mr. Washington's gun? He said that he has a fully loaded revolver already unpacked and under the mattress. I just want to make sure that it has not been fired and has six peas in the shooter. And I don't want you to think I am flirting with the…what was it again? The attractive, helpful, potential suspect, potential witness, reporter of the recently deceased."

A broad smile swept across Pont's face.

"Yeah, I guess I can do that for you before I go to the hospital so you don't have to face that arduous task."

# CHAPTER 15

# ANTHONY GRASSO

*Front yard*
*Four days before the killing*

"Hello, Mr. Happy, how are your dogs doing today?"

A gleeful salutation shouted from the street to Anthony as he placed his merchandise in the back of the big boxy trailer in preparation for this week's trade show.

Anthony grunted and rolled his eyes in response to the question, remembering the threat made by Natalie's father if he were ever to speak to his family ever again, much less his precious little daughter.

*Oh my god, that ignoramus is so irksome. Why must she persistently blab at me? Doesn't she get the hint that I don't want to speak to her? No, because she is a fool. I can't stand the sight of her. Just look at her,* he thought to himself as he made himself angrier and angrier.

The conversation was all one-sided because it was all in his head.

*Doesn't she own a mirror? All I want to do is lop off her unkempt ponytail! Who on earth would wear a skirt with bright-pink flamingos standing in turquoise-colored grass patches with a red-and-black Special Olympics T-shirt? And those long socks with dog heads everywhere and those crazy sequined shoes? Come on!*

He answered his own question inwardly.

*An ignoramus, that's who. She looks utterly ridiculous! Where is her mother when she is walking out the door like that? Isn't her brother ashamed to go to the same school? Does no one care what her appearance says about her? It's ludicrous. I bet the only reason she talks to me is to get under my skin. Why does she call me Mr. Happy all the time? That makes me insane. I wish I could tell her to knock it off, but that would only encourage her to talk to me more and sic her crazy father on me. Yeah, it's best just to ignore her for fear she may come over and try to set up a playdate with my dogs.*

"Mr. Happy, I have to wash my hands now. Got to go, buffalo."

Natalie waves a thin plastic grocery bag loaded with dog poop in the air.

"Say hello to your dogs for me."

*She's probably saving that crap to put on my front door step and flaunting it in my face. She probably collects it and gives it to her brother. He's probably the culprit that puts it on my step. If I catch them, I'll throw it at them like a dung grenade. No, I will hold them down and rub it in their faces. I can't stand that girl or her brother. Yeah, she's probably the one. Her fake friendly behavior. It's all a sham. That girl takes the cake.*

He shuttered to think of her.

*She is too sticky sweet to be real. I wonder if it is all an act. How could anyone be so oblivious?"*

Anthony's final thoughts eventually trailed away from the innocent young lady, and he returned to the task at hand, packing the trailer and readying his wares for the road show.

CHAPTER 16

# DARIUS AND NITA WASHINGTON

*Two nights before the killing*
*On the way home from the bonfire*

"Good night. Thanks for coming," a final shout of farewell.

"Thank you again for having us and making us feel so welcome to the neighborhood," Nita returned the pleasantries over her shoulder as she clung to her husband for stability.

"Careful on your way out. It is a lot easier getting over here than going home. The fire guides you on the way in, but only the moonlight helps you on the way out. The woods keep it pretty dark, and the critters that live there have the advantage of sight. Do you have a flashlight on your phone you can use? I don't want you to break your neck on the way home."

"Good idea. Thanks for the suggestion."

Darius raised his hand carrying the phone with the bright light shining, pointed toward the fire to show that they were now safe from tripping face first into an unsuspecting orange tree or misplaced garden hose.

In a whisper, Nita asked, "What was with you tonight, baby? You weren't your usual outgoing self."

Darius whispered in a harsh edged tone, "Ssh! Can't it wait until we get home?"

Nita had her husband in a tight grip. With only the one flashlight pointed directly in front of Darius's feet, she could not see one step in front of her own. She didn't want to step on a snake or any other obstacle hidden in Kraus's side yard.

They had to go the long way around their new neighbor's house because the closest path, as the crow flies, was obstructed by a small fenced-in area just large enough for the dogs to go to the bathroom and the boat to be hidden away from view. Then there was that barrier of bushes that was so thick and so tall that it was more like a wall, impenetrable. The distant moonlight wasn't going to provide much help this night with the cloud coverage so thick, so she clutched onto her husband as if her life depended on it.

"Oh, nobody can hear us, babe. I noticed you wouldn't look at me when we were talking about my dream. Is that what's bothering you, that I didn't tell you about my second dream?"

"Naw, I mean that was a little weird because you shared your dream with people you just met, and I, I know you think your Bapi was sending you a vision, but that's not what's bugging me really."

She whispered softly, "Then just tell me."

"Well, I'll tell you what's bothering me, but I never want to talk about it again. Promise me. Never again. I can't believe I even have to tell you why. You should already know."

"I swear to you I will never bring it up again. What's eating at you? Does it have to do with what happened in Atlanta?"

Out of earshot, he raised his voice slightly. "Yes, babe! I can't explain it to you any other way than to say being arrested was humiliating. I never want to lose control like that again. I am ashamed that I let that man get to me like that. I am ashamed that I resorted to violence like that. I have always prided myself as being a peaceful man. Or at least I thought I was until it happened twice. I don't know what overcame me, but that force was strong. It seems like it's getting worse for me to handle. I sure as hell didn't want that problem to follow me here. That whole conversation about killing that man made me feel uneasy."

"Babe, they were just trying to make you feel more comfortable about what happened with Mr. Happy."

"Now you're going to start calling that cracker Mr. Happy too? I can think of a few other choice names I could call him."

The conversation was just working Darius up, and he prided himself on keeping his cool.

"I think that's the point. If we use the flippant name, we don't have to take him so seriously."

"Anyway, babe, I felt the same rage when Anthony said that to us, to me, as the night I almost beat a man unconscious."

The contemplative conversation momentarily paused the walking, and he took the time to just breathe.

"Even though he had it coming, I lost control of myself. I am better than that. Or so I thought, but those same feelings came rushing back to me, and I wanted to beat that man too. It took everything I could muster not to react immediately."

He resumed walking slowly again.

"I'm also embarrassed that I lost my job from going to jail that night. As you well know, I could have easily lost my teaching certificate for a breach of moral turpitude. Jail is no place I ever want to return to and no place I want anyone to find out that I have been. It's a damn good thing I had a winning football record and that my previous principal loved me."

"You're the best coach. Everybody loves you, your principal, your students, the other coaches, the other teachers. I love you. Harmony High School is truly lucky to have you as their coach."

"You don't understand. I am a tinderbox. Anthony is the flint. The man can set me off as sure as striking a spark."

"Finally, terra firma under our feet."

The black asphalt of the street steadied their gait, and the lamppost lit their final path home, but they remained locked in an embrace. It was Darius who needed Nita's support not to stumble rather than the other way around. He kissed the top of her head and allowed a tear to roll down his rough exterior.

"It would kill me if it ever got out, Nita. I can't let that shame follow me to St. Cloud. It was the worst time in my life, and I can't go through something like that again. You need to keep me away from that man so I don't screw up the rest of my life, so I won't screw up the rest of our lives."

# CHAPTER 17

# OLD FOLKS TALKING

*Group text message screenshot*
*The day of the killing*

Sat, Sept. 27, 5:20 p.m.

MINDY MOUNTS
We are eating dinner now. We will see you
after it gets dark.

NICK MOUNTS
I picked up a six-pack.

RON KRAUS
Okay, guys, looking forward to seeing you
soon.

\*\*\*\*\*

Mon, Sept. 29, 8:17 a.m.

JOYCE KRAUS
OMG, OMG, OMG! You guys need to
call me.
I have news I should not write in a text.

Hello, gang! Anybody out there?

Why the radio silence? I am freaking out!

Anthony's dead, and the police came into
the house asking questions.

\*\*\*\*\*

Mon, Sept. 29, 9:03 a.m.

RON KRAUS
Sorry, hon, I was in a meeting until the
police came and interrupted me too. They
came to my work! I am guessing that you
will want to talk about them paying you a
visit this morning? I can't talk now. I'll call
you as soon as I can. Don't put anything
else down in writing!

\*\*\*\*\*

Mon, Sept. 29 10:11 a.m.

MINDY MOUNTS
What? We slept in. I am just seeing this.
Nick is out the door already. Did you tell
them about anything? Did you mention
what we talked about at the bonfire?

JOYCE KRAUS
No, call me.

\*\*\*\*\*

Mon, Sept. 29 12:45 p.m.

NICK MOUNTS
I am late to the party as usual. I agree
with Ron. No more texting. No calls. We
will come over tonight after work. Now
radio silence. Text messages can be used
as evidence against you!
Don't talk to the new neighbors.

# CHAPTER 18

# REED KRAUS

*Afternoon of the killing*
*Harmony High School*

A tall, thin, handsome young man with bright blue eyes and clean-cut dark-brown hair presented his admin pass to the secretary in the front office. She pointed to the detective sitting in the chairs lined against the front windows, time-stamped his pass, and returned it to him without a word all the while jotting notes and listening to someone on the other end of the telephone.

"Reed Kraus, I presume?"

"Yes, sir."

Reed extended his hand to greet the policeman. He remembered the advice his mother told him as a young middle school boy.

"Always be the first to extend your hand, especially with adults. It will set you apart from the others. I know this isn't how other kids operate, but it will make you more comfortable in the adult world well before the other kids are admitted. Trust that it will put you on good footing and be to your advantage."

Standing up, the boy towered over the five-foot, eight-inch detective.

"I am Detective Pontonero from the St. Cloud Police Department. What took you so long getting here?"

Annoyed, he lost his usual polite tone with this kid when introducing himself for the first time. Pontonero studied the school clock on the wall as the second hand loudly clicked as time passed with a pregnant pause.

"You were summoned here fifteen minutes ago."

The detective's irritation was clear. Reed must be contrite when talking to this man.

"I am truly sorry. I was finishing lunch. They never told me a policeman was here to see me. I just thought it was the attendance officer. I figured I was in trouble again for skipping my first period class. I thought I was going to get lunch detention, so I was hanging out with my friends until after the first lunch was over. I would rather miss English class than lunch with my friends."

Pontonero sighed deeply. "Okay, I forgive you. That makes sense."

He was still annoyed, but he seemed like an upstanding kid with a humble yet confident air about him. He seemed extraordinarily comfortable talking to an adult much less a detective. Even most adults got nervous after he introduced himself as a law enforcement agent. You catch more flies with honey than vinegar after all.

"I didn't want you talking to your sister before I spoke to her."

"My sister?" Reed said, bewildered about what could possibly be happening. Straight forward yet still maintaining a courteous tone, he asked, "What am I doing here? Respectfully, what is all of this about, sir?"

"Detective," Pontonero corrected. "I need to ask you and your sister a few questions. Do you need your parents here for a few questions?"

It was a good question to cover oneself legally but also baiting the adolescent, appealing to Reed's bravado. No, this kid wasn't going to ask the protection of Mommy and Daddy.

"I guess that depends."

This kid was smart. He didn't fall for the trap.

Reed answered earnestly but calmly, "Please tell me what you are talking about. I have no idea what this could possibly be about. You are getting me amped up."

"Okay, I will get right to the point. You already confirmed something for me. Why did you miss your first period class?"

"It was just journalism or yearbook class. My teacher doesn't care if we miss class, as long as our work's done."

Pontonero looked blankly at the student so that he would elaborate.

"If we have our pictures turned in for the yearbook, we just hang out. Heck, a lot of the kids in the class are out roaming the halls hoping to take pictures of their friends goofing around so they can be in pictures of the yearbook. My mom is the hard one to convince to skip class, but she let me skip so that she could help me study for my biology test. I guess she cares about my grades more than my attendance record."

"How did you do on the test?"

"I aced it." A grin creeped across Reed's face. "I mean I haven't gotten the grade yet, but I just know."

Reed was feeling more comfortable now that the detective was acting less uptight.

"Anthony Grasso died this morning in his driveway. Did you happen to see him or notice anyone out of the usual?"

"What? That's insane!"

Reed stared at Detective Pontonero for a moment to let the news sink in before he realized that the detective had asked him a question.

"No, Dad and sis were gone by the time we left, and it was daylight, but I really wasn't paying attention to anything but the index cards. Mom was driving. I was still reviewing my vocabulary words for bio."

"Okay, Reed. Thank you for your time. You can go back to your riveting English class now."

"Detective, has anyone told you that my sister has special needs?"

"Yes, I am aware that she rode the exceptional education bus to school and that she's doing her internship in the cafeteria and that she's allowed to stay at school until she's twenty-two. That's why I am waiting for the second period lunch to end to speak with her. I can wait until the lunch rush is over," Detective Pontonero said, demonstrating his flexibility.

"Yes, all that is true, but more importantly, did anyone tell you that she is also on the autistic spectrum?"

"What are you trying to tell me, son?"

"Well, with a person who is mentally handicapped, you can't lead them at all because they will tell you what you *trick* them into saying rather than telling what actually happened or the truth. But with a person who has autism, if you say the wrong thing, you could upset them for a very long time after. The slightest thing could set them off. Do you have experience with people with autism?"

"Son, I am an old man. I have encountered all walks of life in my thirty-four years on the job. I will be very courteous when I speak to your sister. Is she afraid of police officers?"

"No, she's not afraid of the police. She actually wants to be a police officer and get the bad guys."

They both smiled at this comment.

"My mom told her she can't have a gun or the bad guy will steal hers and shoot her."

"Great career advice," he concurred.

"She's an innocent girl. She can't even handle hearing cuss words in our home. We can only watch scary or violent TV shows after she goes to bed. And she keeps the fan running in her bathroom so she can't hear anything. My parents won't even allow violent video games in the house because Natalie will wig out. I have to go to my friends' houses to play any fun video games. She won't let any of us in our family say an unkind word about anyone, including a jerk like Mr. Happy. Our dogs died a few years ago, and she still perseverates on it daily, to this day. So what I am saying is, can you please not tell her anything about him dying and just ask questions that are not leading?"

"You are a bright young man for the little brother. How do you know such a big word as *perseverate*?"

"Unfortunately, it is a common word in our family."

Vibrant, upbeat music piped in the office and blasted out on the patio.

"That is the end of the second lunch period. They don't use bells to change classes here."

"Technically, she's an adult, but I know how fond you are of skipping class. Would you want to stay and make her feel more comfortable?"

Reed's tension visibly eased.

"I thought you would never ask."

# CHAPTER 19

# NITA WASHINGTON

*Afternoon of the killing*
*Home of Nita and Darius Washington*

Nita swung the door open wide. This time, Mrs. Washington was clearly ready to face the day. Her salwar kameez was a deep turquoise with gold embroidery that fell just below the knee and had matching pants that appeared both festive and casual. She wore her silky long, black hair straight down her back with a very sharp edge, waist length. It was freshly cut and well groomed.

This was very much unlike this morning when he first met Mrs. Washington in the victim's driveway, in her bathrobe, without a stitch of makeup and her hair piled on top of her head in a messy bun. This time, Detective Hannon noticed just how stunning Nita Washington was. Her eyeliner lifted in the outer corners, which gave her a very exotic and dramatic look. She wore lipstick that was only slightly more colored than her natural tone to give her already plump lips the attention they deserved. Her lips had two pointed arches that the lipstick defined more sharply and created an effect that he had not noticed earlier. Perhaps it was his lack of coffee or maybe "she just cleans up well," as the saying goes.

"Did I catch you at a bad time? Are you headed for work? It looks like you are all dressed up to go somewhere."

"Hello, Detective... Hannon, was it?"

He nodded in the affirmative.

"No, I'm a yoga instructor, but I haven't started building up new clients just yet. I was going to go out shopping for a bit to get a few things we need for the house and then to the post office to change my address and send a package to my mother. But that can wait. Please come in. Excuse the mess. I haven't pulled the house together completely yet. I was beginning to think you were not coming back like you mentioned this morning."

"I let the investigation lead me. Which led me back to you, Mrs. Washington."

"Oh?" she responded with a surprised confusion.

"I don't mean to make you uncomfortable, ma'am. I just had lunch with my partner, Detective Pontonero. You may remember him from this morning when we first met?"

"Yes, of course, I remember him. I will never forget this morning. Unfortunately for me, the events of this morning will forever be scorched into my memory."

Hannon stepped into the foyer and said, "Detective Pontonero had come from a visit from the high school where your husband works. Do you mind if I look around the place? He mentioned that you own a gun. Mind if I take a look at it?"

Mrs. Washington suddenly had a defensive look about her.

"I can come back with a warrant if you prefer, Mrs. Washington. It's just that your husband mentioned it like I said, and I figured that if *he* brought the revolver up, he wouldn't mind me inspecting it."

"No, of course not. Please feel free to have a look about the entire house. The gun is actually upstairs, in our bedroom, under the mattress. You can take it with you if you like. It has never even been fired. Fortunately for us, we have never had to use it."

"Thank you, Mrs. Washington. Don't be nervous. It is in your best interest really. I just want to rule both you and Coach Washington out as suspects. That's all."

"I am the one that called it in. I didn't think I would be a suspect."

"Honestly, you have nothing to worry about. Just tell me everything you can remember about what happened this morning, including leading up to and how you came across Mr. Grasso?"

Nita led the way up the steps, her hand gracefully slid up the banister as she glanced over her shoulder to see if Detective Hannon was following her. He had given her a wide berth deliberately so that there was an appropriate amount of distance between his face and her posterior.

As they reached the top of the steps, she motioned toward the bedroom and allowed him to enter the room and check for the gun himself as she remained in the doorframe. He put on gloves from his pocket and pulled out a bag.

He quickly found the gun where she told him it would be and said, "I will be borrowing this for a while."

He placed the gun in the bag and zipped it up. He glanced about the room. No decorations were on the walls yet. No knick-knacks were placed about the room, just boxes marked "master bedroom." He peeked in all the upstairs bedrooms. She had a way to go before she would be completely settled in. They descended the stairs. This time, Hannon led the way.

"As I told Detective Pontonero earlier, I had just made breakfast for Darius. He went upstairs to finish getting ready for work. I was trying to clean up the morning dishes when I stumbled over some cardboard boxes. So I decided to stack them by the front door. As I was finishing the dishes and sweeping the kitchen, Darius kissed me goodbye, and I watched him through the front window as he left for work. I saw him wave to Mr. Kraus across the street. I knew it wasn't garbage day, but the clutter inside was difficult to maneuver around and just bugged me, so I began dragging the broken-down boxes out to the curb."

"In your pajamas? When I saw you this morning, you were still in your bathrobe."

He walked around downstairs, looking for anything out of the ordinary.

"It was still dark out. I didn't expect to find a dead neighbor or see any other people, for that matter. It is very private out here. As you can see for yourself, our house is surrounded by woods. I have already seen a family of deer in my yard."

"Did you see any other people?"

"When Darius was leaving, so was Mr. Kraus, but he did not see me. I watched them both from the window."

"Did you see anybody else this morning?"

"I heard a loud school bus rumble by, and it turned around at the end of the street and came back and picked up Mr. Kraus's daughter. I stayed out of sight because I was still in my bathrobe, and I didn't want the kids on the bus to see me indisposed."

"It was still dark out when the bus came. How did you know it was her and not the son?"

"She was standing under the streetlight, waiting for the bus. I could clearly see her. Such a sweetheart. I have never seen anyone so happy to greet her bus driver. She was waving and smiling at all the kids on the bus."

"Did you see anyone else?"

"Yes, I saw the son and wife leave about an hour later. It was getting light out by then. But I was still unpacking dishes and pots and pans in my bathrobe. I had not showered yet. I made a few trips to the curb. Each time I emptied a box, I brought it to the curb to get it out from under my feet and see the progress I was making. My mother used to always tell me 'clean as you go.'"

"Did you see Anthony pull into the driveway this morning?"

"No, I didn't notice exactly when he pulled in. I was in and out. I was busy unpacking and moving things around in various cabinets and drawers. He may have been there for a couple of my trips. I didn't notice anything off right away because I was in my own little world."

"Is this the garage? Do you mind if we exit through the garage?"

She followed Detective Hannon down three small steps into the garage where her 2016 turquoise Chevy Spark was kept. That was a reasonable car for a teacher and yoga instructor to own. He made a mental note but was surprised by such a large house and in this neighborhood. Alongside of her car was a weight bench, presumably for her husband, and various boxes labeled "garage."

"So what made you go across the street to find Mr. Grasso?"

"The truck door was ajar with a dinging sound repeating, and the lights were on. That went on probably longer than it should have before I noticed. You know how you hear something for a while until it finally registers?"

Hannon nodded so she would continue.

"But it wasn't until it started getting lighter when I looked more closely. I noticed the blood-soaked bricks first. I called out to him a few times, and he obviously could not answer. I was reluctant to have him see me in my robe, but eventually, I walked around the trailer and truck to find him in a crumpled heap. That's when I ran back inside to grab my cell phone and rang 911. I was a bit rattled. I couldn't even remember the name of my street at first. The 911 operator made me check for his pulse, but it was too late. He was already gone."

Nita was visibly worked up again. Her face got red, her hands began shaking, and her voice seemed to go up an octave.

"I ran back over to stay with him until the police arrived. There was a man and a woman police officer. The policeman never spoke to me. The woman just asked me to step back. She didn't talk to me too much. The woman was asking me my name, and where I lived, and told me to calm down because I was crying."

She put both her hands and palms outward.

"But I had never seen a dead body before, especially with so much blood. There was so much blood. Then the other detective, Pontonero, arrived shortly after and took my statement. He was much more friendly and kind than the lady police officer. He spoke to me gently, you know? That really helped me calm down. Not like that lady police officer telling me to 'calm down.' Does that ever work? Telling an upset person to calm down? Finally, you arrived and asked me to go home and wait to reiterate what happened, and here we are."

"That wasn't so bad, was it? Just a couple of more questions. We are finished up here. Do either you or your husband hunt?"

To this remark, Nita scoffed. "No, Detective," she addressed Hannon directly into his aging eyes. Her voice softened. "I am

Hindu. We are vegetarians. I believe in karma. I don't want Vishnu to make me a cockroach in my next life. We would never take a life."

"So your husband is Hindu also?"

"No. He is Baptist. He believes 'Thou shalt not kill.'"

"That leads me to the bonfire. Why didn't you mention to my partner that you were all talking about killing Anthony Grasso at the party?"

"I didn't think it was relevant. I was just trying to fit in with the new neighbors. It was all a big joke. The woman started asking people how we would murder him because he drove everyone mad, and it was just fun, liberating."

"Mrs. Kraus?"

"No, the other woman, Mindy Mounts."

"Just out of curiosity, how did you hypothetically murder him?"

"I bumped him off with my car. Huh! Get it, the pun, bumper of a car?"

"I do now. I find it a tad inappropriate to make a joke about it now that he is actually dead, ma'am."

Her short-lived smile disappeared into a contrite look toward her feet.

"You are absolutely right. I apologize."

"Thank you for inviting me into your home and for calling in the emergency, Mrs. Washington. You have been most helpful. Enjoy the rest of your day."

Detective Hannon's kind words belied his stern expression, leaving Mrs. Washington feeling uneasy with their interaction.

# CHAPTER 20

# LEIGH AND REED

*Ten days before the killing*
*The Krauses' driveway*

"What's the matter with you?"

Leigh was standing outside of the running vehicle under the streetlamp. Leigh threw both of his hands to his crotch to indicate a large wet spot.

"Did you piss yourself?"

"No, man, I didn't piss myself." He mocked the phrase back to Reed in a derisive voice to reveal how upset he was. "Your freaking neighbor did this to me!"

"WHAT?"

Leigh excitedly recounted the story. "Yeah, I was pulling into your driveway jamming out trying to set the vibe for the day, and he started yelling something. So I turned the music down to hear what was getting the old fart's panties in a knot, and he started cussing at me about my music being too loud and threw an old Big Gulp at me."

Reed's eyes grew wide. "What did you do?"

"I threw my Jeep into park, jumped out, and chased him back to his little cave."

Leigh raked his fingers through his ample hair. The more he thought about it, the angrier he got.

"I say we go drag him out of his house and deliver him a sufficient beat down."

"Naw, man." In a very soothing and calming voice, Reed quietly asked, "What do they say about revenge?"

Leigh crossed his arms and leaned back against his Jeep disappointed to hear his friend try to be the voice of reason.

"The best revenge is a good life lived well?"

"Yeah...," Reed said, nodding his head, "if you are an old woman." Reed started smirking. "Remember in language arts class when we all had to memorize different quotes about revenge and explain them to each other?"

Leigh nodded that he did.

"My quote was from Albert Einstein, who said, 'Weak people revenge, strong people forgive, intelligent people ignore.'"

Leigh shook his head in disbelief at his friend's reaction. He was looking for support not wisdom.

In a goofy, fake, hillbilly accent, Reed joked, "We some weak dummies who gonna get us some vengeance."

Reed playfully slapped his friend on his chest.

"No, man. We aren't in language arts or philosophy class today, brother. I got your back. I was thinking of the saying, 'Revenge is a dish best served cold.' Get in the Jeep and 'play that funky music, White boy.' Your pants will dry before we get to school, and no chicks will think you tinkled in your pants. Come on now, turn it up!"

# CHAPTER 21

# NATALIE KRAUS

*The afternoon of the killing*
*Harmony High School*

"Say hello to your dogs for me!" a disembodied voice shouted from down the hall. Her voice preceded her.

"That's my sister. You can hear her from a mile away," Reed informed Detective Pontonero with a smile on his face.

She noticed Reed immediately before making it all the way to the front office.

"Brother!" Natalie shouted too loudly inside an office building, throwing her arms around her little brother. She was oblivious to anyone else in the room.

"Sister," Reed responded, returning the salutation and love, albeit more quietly.

Natalie was a happy girl with chubby cheeks and had the curse of the lunchroom lady already. She was still wearing the hairnet and her black apron over the top of her black-and-royal-blue uniform with the sensible no-skid shoes, which made her look frumpy and older than the detective expected. Her flawless, pale skin was like porcelain and the only indication that she was quite young. She was dark haired with bangs and wore tortoise shell glasses. Her sweet personality shone the moment she entered the room. Pontonero couldn't help but like her immediately.

He had an affinity for people with special needs and always supported the torch run every year by chipping in fifty bucks. The police force in Osceola County were major backers of the Special Olympics, and every year, the young, fit police officers ran to raise money. He made it a point to cheer them on as he was well past his years of running in the event.

"Hello, Natalie," Detective Pontonero interrupted the family reunion.

"Hello," Natalie noticed the other man in the small side office adjacent to the front office where Reed and he had moved for more privacy. The front office started filling up with parents and students being checked out of school for various doctor's appointments, which happened every school afternoon, and this day was no different than any other. The attendance monitor was no longer using the office as he was out on the golf cart putting out cones in the student parking lot getting ready for dismissal.

"How has your day been going so far?"

"Fine, the principal just gave me a mint."

As she unwrapped it, she smiled, self-satisfied, and popped it in her mouth.

"You want me to get you one? The principal loves me, and I can get a mint for you if you want."

With a chuckle, Pontonero politely declined. "No, thank you."

Reed shook his head as well.

"Can you tell me about your morning?"

"Sure, I broke down the boxes and took them out to the dumpster. I washed the apples and put them in plastic bags. I filled up the cups of cheese."

"Yes, that's wonderful. It sounds like you worked hard today. But can you tell me what happened before school started? Could you start with when you woke up this morning?"

"Yes. Daddy and I walked the dogs. Usually, I walk with Reed but not today. He was studying. So I walked with Dad. Hehe."

She had a funny laugh, and she started clapping quietly over her mouth. She clearly enjoyed the attention of her father.

"You walked the dogs in the dark?"

"Yes, we used the flashlights on our phones, and Dad had his hunting lamp on his head."

Reed added, "Yeah, Dad wears his hunting lamp on his head when he walks the dogs in the dark. Mom thinks it looks dorky, but he doesn't care. He kind of looks like a coal miner."

"Did you see any neighbors while you were on your walk?" Pontonero returned to Natalie.

"No. Everyone was asleep in their houses."

"So you did not see Anthony Grasso?"

Natalie looked confused. "Who's that?"

Reed interjected, "He's talking about Mr. Happy."

"No, he wasn't home yet," Natalie said, shaking her head.

"Yet? Did you see Mr. Happy come home? Did you see him today?"

His voice turned a little intense suddenly.

"No." She took a step back away from the officer. "We went inside and ate breakfast. But when I got on the bus, I heard his truck running, and all the lights were on in his truck. His bell was dinging. Am I in trouble or something?" Natalie spoke a bit more softly than before.

"So you never saw Mr. Happy today?" Detective Pontonero reiterated for clarity.

"Nope. Was I supposed to?"

"No, sweetheart, just checking." He spoke more gently, realizing his mistake.

"Do you have dogs?" Natalie switched the subject to her favorite topic. "I have two. Well, four, actually, if you count the ones that died. Hagrid and Hermione are buried in the backyard. Hagrid was sixteen, and he died of old age, but Hermione was sick."

Reed gave the detective a meaningful look, hoping the detective recalled his previous conversation.

"No, I'm more of a cat person myself. I have one tabby at home. Thank you, Natalie. You have been quite helpful."

Detective Pontonero smiled at Reed. "How did I do?"

"You aced it."

Reed fist-bumped the officer in appreciation for the tender line of questioning.

"Come on, sis, you can walk me back to class. Maybe you can score another mint from the principal's office for me."

Reed led his sister out the door with his arm loosely draped across her shoulder.

## CHAPTER 22

# NICK MOUNTS

*The day following the killing*
*The Mounts residence*

Loud banging on the front door startled Nick and interrupted him from a deep sleep.

"What the heck? Stop banging!" Nick screamed at whoever was pounding on the door, causing his dogs to howl and his heart to race.

He checked his phone to decide whether or not he was going to get out of bed to answer the door or go back to sleep. The camera on his phone clearly showed two old men in dated suits. They weren't going away any time soon, so he slipped on an old, faded white snake T-shirt and a pair of faded, threadbared jeans with a hole forming at the knee and headed for the front door.

"Wait a minute!" he yelled at his visitors to let them know that he was annoyed at this disturbance.

He reoriented himself to put his three, overly excited dogs in the backyard so he could get some peace from their constant yapping. In his groggy state, the dogs were more annoying than usual and kept his heart rate elevated.

"Can I help you?" he greeted the officers in a not-so-friendly tone.

He already had a run-in with the police in a case of mistaken identity as a younger man. It ended up with him lying facedown in the middle of a dirty convenience store floor and a police knee on the back of his neck. It bore out soon that they had the wrong man in cuffs for an armed robbery where he had matched the description, a six-foot Caucasian male with dirty-blond hair, driving a 2009 orange-and-black Challenger. Before long, he was standing upright, dusted off, and apologized to when it was heard over the police radio the correct suspect had been apprehended, cuffed, and stuffed.

That humiliating incident left a bad taste in his mouth for the police. Nick had a couple of speeding violations but otherwise was an upstanding citizen, a pillar of the business community even. The Mounts had given their time, talents, and treasures to various causes since their company started becoming prosperous.

During the last couple of hurricanes, Nick and his sons personally led a small crew of employees to feed victims, as well as first responders to those in need after the devastation of Hurricane Irma and Hurricane Michael.

Schools always loved to motivate their students with pizza parties. For years, the couple had given out free coupons to countless schools in three of the counties where they owned restaurants. Mr. and Mrs. Mounts had cooked and donated every year for camps for children with cancer.

Currently, human trafficking had become a horrible problem in the Central Florida area, and the Mounts were focusing on this problem as their charity of choice this year. Education seemed to be a first step in tackling this epidemic.

Nick was a good man, a fun friend, and fiercely loyal to those he loved but a frightening man to those who were not permitted inside his inner circle. He was handsome but looked hard and mean as a snake when his ire was raised.

"Yes, sir, we want to talk to you about the death of your neighbor Anthony Grasso. Do you mind if we step inside the house?"

"You can step in, but we can talk right here in my foyer."

Nick said this with his arms folded and his stance wide. These detectives were going to have to work hard to get anything from this hard-edged man. The previous encounter with the police left an indelible mark on him, and he no longer had a trusting opinion of them. He knew that Mr. and Mrs. Kraus had already been interviewed yesterday because they had an ongoing group text message, and both of them had mentioned it right after it occurred. He knew it was a matter of time before they would come speak to them. A strong wave of dog smell filled their lungs as they entered the home.

"Is your wife at home? We would like to speak with both of you if possible."

"No, she had a business meeting in Orlando this morning," Nick said, still stoic, arms crossed, and on guard.

"Wow, this is impressive," one of the detectives said, touching the lacquered wooden scabbard of the weapon displayed. "Is this a real samurai sword or just a replica for show?"

The detective knew exactly what he was doing. He disarmed this hard-boiled man by finding his weakness or more precisely his obsession.

"It is one of my finest and most expensive pieces. It is an ancient Japanese katana. Today, the blades are made of Swedish powdered steel. But not this beauty. This particular samurai sword is over six hundred years old. It was made from iron ore and has been forged and folded over and over again by a Japanese swordsmith to remove all the impurities. The newer ones are probably stronger, but just look at the craftsmanship of this blade. It is a one of a kind, not like the ones today that have a stamp on the side, marking which batch it came from. See the pattern on the edge. That was created with fire. This one is a feudal era sword. The Japanese stone polished the blade for days, if not weeks. This handle is long enough to accommodate both hands."

He picked up the fourteenth-century sword with two hands, prompting both detectives to step back and reach for their guns. Nick, observant of the tension, quickly returned the sword to its proper place so as not to have a repeat of his previous experience.

The detective was successful at putting the man before him at ease. The fervent interest the detectives demonstrated in the collection of knives earned them more trust and respect and would possibly lead to a more fruitful line of questioning. Nick lost his defensive attitude that he had when they first stepped into his home. He clearly could have elaborated more about his collection, but for now, the detectives are more focused on his alibi and his motivation for possibly killing the victim. They had already checked to see if the Mounts had any outstanding warrants, which both Nick and Mindy did not have, and were well aware of their clean records.

"You don't seem surprised by our visit," Detective Hannon began the line of questioning.

It was more of a statement than a question really, but it prompted a response from Mr. Mounts.

"Yeah, our friends told us that you talked to them already. We assumed that you may stop by here as well."

"We understand that there was a bonfire this weekend, and Anthony Grasso was the subject of most of the discussion."

"Yes, I knew that you had already heard what we were joking about."

Truth be told, he thought that his friends were smart enough not to mention the bonfire. But he wanted the police to think he was up to speed on everything that was discussed with them.

"Admittedly, I had a few beers. We were just unwinding, trying to find out what happened to our new neighbors. You know, making Coach more comfortable after he had been threatened like that. Apparently, Anthony was his usual jackass self and said some rude remark to scare the Washingtons into submission."

"We heard," Pontonero redirected the interview back toward Nick and his wife's part of the story. "What made your wife bring up killing Anthony as the main event of the party?"

"Did she? I don't remember who started talking about that first."

He crossed his arms across his chest again, resuming a more distrustful stance.

"It was your wife, according to our notes," Detective Hannon revealed.

"My wife is the kindest, most loving woman you would ever want to meet, Detective...?" Nick wanted to catch the last name to remember.

"Detective Hannon," he reminded him.

"Detective Hannon, in her mind, she was just a momma bear defending her cubs."

The detectives stared at Nick, expecting him to continue.

"It started with Anthony catching my boys toilet papering his yard years ago when they were in middle school. They used to ride their RipStiks and bikes in front of his house because that is the only place Mindy would allow the kids to play unsupervised. There was absolutely no traffic because at that time, only two families lived down there, and it was the safest place to play. But Anthony hates kids. I should rephrase that. Anthony hates everybody, but he picks on people he thinks he can push around. So they became the perfect target. Too small to fight back at a man screaming and cursing at them twice their size. He started a war with teenagers, and they have way more energy to keep the war going. So they started hounding him by soaping his windows and writing, 'Mr. Happy, why you gotta be so mean?'"

He started laughing and rubbing his chin, reflecting over the memory.

"Hell, to be honest with you, I bought extra toilet paper for the boys to toss in his trees. But that is as far as it went. The boys grew older, and when they started driving, they no longer came into contact with the grouch. They started getting new interests in girls, cars, and work, so they lost interest in retaliation with Mr. Happy. The problem is, Anthony continued to harbor hate toward our sons and spread rumors every chance he could. But anyone and everyone who has come into contact with the man knows he's full of piss and vinegar."

Detective Pontonero knew these things were small potatoes and, while being irritating, didn't seem like any path to murder. He forced the conversation away from Momma Bear Mindy and explored Nick's possible motivation for killing Mr. Grasso.

"So, Nick, have you ever had a confrontation directly with Mr. Grasso?"

"Who hasn't? To know him is to hate him. So yes, I've had a confrontation with the man. He goes around kicking over garbage cans if people put them out early, so when he was heading to my can,

I yelled at him. He stared me down hard, so I said if he touched my garbage cans, I would slice his hands off and stuff them in his garbage cans. He's just a blowhard, but when it comes down to it, he's all talk and no action. He's only good at intimidating women, children, and the elderly."

"The elderly? Who did he bully that was old?"

"There used to be an old traditional Pakistani couple or maybe Indian couple that lived across the street from Anthony. He harassed those poor immigrants endlessly. He would call them dot heads and vile things so harmful and disgusting I don't even want to repeat them. Really and truly the most hateful things you've ever heard, so despicable I'm uncomfortable thinking about it. The old woman told my wife that he dumped his garbage in their backyard to frighten them. It must've worked too because she said was moving back home, wherever that was, because he scared them so much."

"Well, I doubt that we'll be hearing from them. Not likely that they are credible suspects as they've moved out of the country and are elderly as you said."

Pont looked around the house. The house was an open plan with the kitchen, dining room, and living room one big open area. It was possible to see the majority of the home minus the bedrooms tucked away in each corner.

"Do you own a weapon, Mr. Mounts?"

Laughing, he said, "You mean other than all the ones you have been looking at since you've gotten here? Yes, I own guns, just like any red-blooded American."

Nick scoffed and shook his head at the question.

"Do you mind if I take a look at them?" Pontonero asked while Detective Hannon took a couple of photos of the extensive knife collection.

The untrusting man, Nick said, "Do you have a warrant?"

"Do I need one?" Pontonero fired back.

"You do if you want to see my guns or get past my foyer."

Hannon inquired, "Mr. Mounts, where were you yesterday morning between 5:00 and 6:00 a.m.?"

"Normally, I would be sleeping next to my beautiful wife. But one of my stores in Kissimmee had an oven go out, and we had to swap them out before the store opened. You can ask the store manager. My wife and I were both there, along with the manager and another employee," he lied.

"Thank you, Mr. Mounts."

Detective Hannon unfolded his notebook to a blank page and gave it to the willing man.

"If you could just write down their names and phone numbers and addresses, we'll let you go back to sleep. Sorry to have disturbed you."

"I am up now. How could I go back to sleep now?"

He checked his cell phone to obtain the phone numbers of his manager and employee and the address he knew by heart.

"Nice collection. Hopefully, you will never need to use any of these blades. The next time we visit, it will be with a warrant."

Not bothering to hide his annoyance, Nick opened the door for the detectives and stood out on the porch until the undercover vehicle backed out of the winding driveway and exited the neighborhood out of sight.

# CHAPTER 23

# JANINE STADLER

*Kissimmee General Hospital*
*The evening after the killing*

"Nurse Stadler?"

A pleasant-looking African American woman in her fifties sat behind a modest desk with black hair that started to gray at her temples. She had large, soft brown eyes that made her look like an empathetic and caring nurse. Her warm smile welcomed the detective before her words.

"Please come in. You can shut the door for privacy," she said, closing the chart she held in her hands, laying it aside for now.

"I spoke to you on the phone briefly yesterday. I have an appointment with you."

She nodded and beckoned him inside the tiny office with her first two fingers without interrupting him.

"I am Detective Hannon. Thank you for taking the time out of your busy schedule to talk with me."

"No problem, Detective. Please have a seat."

There was only room enough for one very industrial-looking, straight-backed, hard chair.

"How can I help you?"

She didn't rush the detective despite having a pile of medical charts piled on her desk and a busy hospital to run.

The ring of the phone interrupted the investigation.

"I'm sorry. This phone never rests."

She held up her finger while listening to the emergency.

"Did you call security yet? Okay, just for good measure, send an orderly for backup, just in case."

As she hung up the receiver, Mrs. Stadler explained the situation to the detective while shaking her head.

"An escaped Baker Acted patient is running around the property with nothing on but his hospital-issued gown. No undies."

With this, they both smiled.

"As I stated on the phone yesterday, I wanted to check on one of your employees, Amanda Grasso."

"Amanda?"

She was surprised that the employee that a policeman was here to discuss was Amanda.

She delved right in because of her busy schedule.

"She's a good nurse, smart, kind of quiet. Her patients seem to like her. She gets along well with the other employees. Amanda is quick to lend a hand for those who need help. She's reliable and seldom calls in to miss work, and when she does call in sick, it is usually for her son, when he's ill. What do you want to know beyond that?"

She was very to the point, and he appreciated that, and thoroughly descriptive for not understanding the gravity of the situation as of yet.

"Can you tell me her work schedule this past week?"

Detective Hannon was in the business of getting information, not giving it, so he doesn't want to reveal anything too soon. Even though he only needed to know about yesterday, he wanted to see her routine. People were creatures of habit, and patterns ruled everyone's behavior. When patterns were disrupted, that was how and when detectives solve cases, like calling in sick perhaps or broken routines.

"Amanda works the night shift, so that means she arrives at 7:00 p.m. and doesn't leave the hospital until 7:00 a.m. She works four days on, three days off. Let's see."

Nurse Stadler tilted her head back to look through the lower part of her bifocals at the wall right next to her. There hung a huge dry-erase chart with various names written with various colors of Vis-a-vis markers. In her hands, she held a paper copy as well that included the same schedule but for the entire month, not just this week.

She tapped the board where it said *Grasso* in bright green indicating Sunday, Monday, Tuesday, Wednesday. She highlighted the name Grasso on her paper and provided the copy to Detective Hannon.

"You can have that copy. I have it on my computer."

He thumbed through the pages and noted it was just as Nurse Stadler had mentioned, four days of work, three days off to spend with her son.

He wondered to himself silently, *It must have been difficult to maintain a sleep schedule when you are the only parent at home with a fifteen-year-old boy around to keep the boy on track.*

"My computer is cabled to the television. I can pull it up on the screen if you prefer?"

She was reaching for the remote control when Detective Hannon declined her offer.

"No, that won't be necessary. I'm old school. I like things handwritten on the board better."

They shared a moment and a laugh.

"I thought I was the only one. The administration wasted their money on this TV in my office."

This comment endeared Nurse Stadler to the aging detective.

The phone rang again, and Nurse Stadler shrugged at the detective as she answered the call.

"Well, thank you for notifying me. I will come down shortly to sign the paperwork."

She tilted her head at the phone while indicating the subject of the call.

"Gunshot wound in the ER."

"What can you tell me about her shift Sunday night?" Hannon pursued his line of questioning.

"She had six patients. Most patients sleep through the night until we have to wake them for medication. Her patients all survived the night. She worked a regular night shift. She's separated from her husband, and her son lives with her, so she called home about 5:45 a.m., you know, to make sure her son is out of bed and getting ready for school. And James Alberti escorted her to her car, as usual, whenever they worked together."

"Is James Alberti the night watchman?"

"Heavens, no. He's another nurse that she is…," she said, tossing her head back and forth, trying to find the right words to describe the relationship, "close to."

"Is that her routine, to call home every morning?"

"Yes. That's routine for her. She has an alarm set on her smartwatch. We all have families. She has permission to call home on her shift. We know our nurses and staff are professional and need to take care of their families too. Amanda calls Charlie every school day since she moved out and away from her awful husband."

"You seem to know her very well."

"Absolutely, we've both worked here for years."

"Have you ever met her husband, Anthony?"

"Yes, unfortunately, I have met the man. What a piece of work that guy is. Did he hurt her?"

She leaned forward as if it were a very real possibility.

The phone interrupted once more.

She answered again and scribbled, "Blood bank out of platelets. Dispatch stat transport from outside facility before next patient."

This time, she didn't even bother explaining the emergency to him.

Noting how busy this woman was, he continued, "No, nothing like that. He did not hurt her. You were saying that you know Anthony?"

"Yes, one year, a few of us were invited over to her house for a few cocktails and appetizers. It was a small Christmas party. It must have been five or six years ago because I wasn't the charge nurse yet and her son, Charlie, was still a little boy. Anyway, when we showed up, Anthony was already three sheets to the wind. I felt so sorry for her and for her son, Charlie. That man was an embarrassment to both of them."

"What exactly happened, Ms. Stadler?"

"Mrs. Stadler," she corrected the detective politely. "He knew we were all nurses. And most of our spouses and family are really proud of us and think of us as healers and angels of mercy. My husband tells me all the time that I am a hero, and these days, I mostly answer phones, do paperwork, and relieve the other nurses so they can go on breaks. But not this jerk of a husband. I didn't even finish my first drink before he started insulting us. Anthony said why don't we all get real jobs? 'Real jobs!'"

She repeated the insult and slapped her palm on her desk, and you could tell by her facial expression that the sting of his words was as fresh today as the day he delivered it.

"He said all we do is clean up other people's 'shit.' Pardon me. His words, not mine. And we didn't need a college degree for that. We could clean toilets and save our parent's college tuition."

The detective looked embarrassed by Anthony's sentiments for her.

"He obviously has a problem with Amanda having more education than he had. Amanda was mortified and begged him to stop, and he told her to 'shut the hell up.' Oh, needless to say, we all left immediately. I guess that was his idea of teaching her a lesson. He escorted us out to the door, calling us 'stuck up――――.' Well, you get the idea. Quite a misogynistic word from a misogynistic man."

Yes, Hannon indeed got the idea.

"Amanda has never invited us since, and I am sure no one would ever go even if she had. So his methods were effective. I don't know how she didn't leave him long ago. We never spoke about that day again in front of her. We didn't want to embarrass her because she is really quite a remarkable nurse and a devoted mother."

"Well, do you know if Amanda has a new relationship in her life since the separation?"

A smile appeared in genuine happiness for her friend and coworker.

"I am not sure he has acted on it, but I think James has an eye for Amanda. He always waits for her when their shift ends and walks her to her car. They often stand very close to one another when checking their charts, and I know flirting when I see it."

She winked at the detective to drive home the point, not to flirt. Finally, the nurse had the courage to inquire.

"May I ask why are you here, Detective Hannon, questioning me about Amanda and her husband? Why are you interested in Amanda's work schedule?"

"Anthony Grasso was killed Monday morning. But you say that she worked Sunday and didn't get off until seven, so it looks like she could not have done it. Did the Alberti chap work by chance yesterday? I don't see his name on the board for yesterday?"

"No, he works Monday, Tuesday, Wednesday, and Thursday this week. See his name in purple."

She tapped the board once more, focused on his name this time. The news left the charge nurse bewildered and lost in thought.

Hannon could not miss the purple lettering. He already mentally noted it when she mentioned him the first time. He was simply confirming that James Alberti, a potential boyfriend of the vic's wife, had the day off from work the day he was killed.

The phone rang again with another crisis.

"Oh my gosh, seriously, the ER is flooded? Well, it's no longer sterile."

Still speaking into the phone, she stood up.

"I have a call tree for the engineers. I will notify them. Then I'll have to reschedule the surgeries that are coming up in the next few hours. Yes, right away, after I notify public relations and risk management about the gunshot wound."

"What a nightmare," Nurse Stadler whispered under her breath.

"I see you have your hands full. Thank you for your time, Mrs. Stadler."

Her eyes glossed over but said nothing in response. He left the door open wide and exited down the corridor without waiting for a goodbye.

C H A P T E R  2 4

# MINDY MOUNTS

*One day after the killing*
*One of the pizza restaurants owned by the Mounts in Kissimmee*

Mindy was an affable woman, liked by all. Her persona was quite the opposite of that of her husband. When it came to their employees, she had a softer approach.

Nick was the hard-nosed, no-nonsense businessman that kept the employees in line, on time, shirts tucked in, and hands out of the till.

While she had a charming, good-natured, down-to-earth sincerity about her that children have, most adults usually lose this by the time they start having their own children. This made her stand out in the crowd. It even earned her accolades among her fellow businessmen and businesswomen in the community. This quality especially endeared her to her many trusted managers.

She groomed a few of her hardest working, most loyal managers to become owners of their stores when they retired in five short years. They wouldn't allow just anyone to buy the profitable business from them. Only the best who proved their allegiance would be entitled to this reward. Fidelity would forever change the course of their destiny.

Rather than long hours and a modest income, ownership and entrepreneurship could transform lives and most certainly put them in a new tax bracket. For this, they gave their undying loyalty to the Mounts, especially Mindy. Over the years grinding out pizzas together, going to conferences, and putting out fires literally and figuratively, Mindy knew without a doubt she could trust her best manager, Esperanza Awilda Hernandez. She had helped install the new oven along with her little brother, who worked for her at that same store in Kissimmee.

Mindy didn't need to explain anything to Esperanza, but she did so because trust works both ways. She relayed that Mindy received a call from two detectives who would be coming by sometime soon to investigate the suspicious death of a neighbor.

Nick called his wife immediately after the detective's home visit to give Mindy the lowdown.

Mindy plainly told Esperanza that Nick lied to the detectives and said that the four of them were here at this store replacing the old oven. Nick believed the police would not accept that they were both sound asleep next to one another as one another's alibi.

He had watched too many *Forensic Files* on television to know that family alibis never worked. Nick felt he needed someone more convincing, outside of the family, to bear witness of his whereabouts on the day Anthony was shot. It would not be too big of a stretch to just change the day from Sunday to Monday. Every other detail would be exactly the same.

"The devil is in the details. Be as precise as you want because it really happened, just one single day differently."

The old oven was, after all, still out by the dumpster, dismantled, but not yet removed from the property.

It was evident to Esperanza that all of their fates rested on this one lie. Her alibi like her loyalty for them was without question. Deep in her heart, she believed Mindy incapable of murder. Nick, on the other hand, left some doubt.

Over the course of the years, she had seen firsthand his quick wrath at the poor employee who forgot their visor at home or the driver seen texting and driving with their logo on the vehicle. Thankfully, this ire was never directed at her. But this was not the point. Whether he was guilty or not, her loyalty would be rewarded by the Mounts, and she knew it. Esperanza was beholden to the Mounts.

## CHAPTER 25

# SHIRLEY PORTER

*Two days after the killing*
*District 9 Medical Examiner's Office*

The boxy, beige, concrete government building was located on the corner of Michigan Avenue and Bumby Avenue in Orlando. The detectives were in a foul mood due to the excessive amount of traffic flowing well below the speed limit. A forty-five-minute drive devolved into an hour-and-fifteen-minute commute during the peak morning rush hour traffic.

"I could not handle living in Orlando. This is madness. You're driving on the way back to St. Cloud."

With that, Hannon slammed the door and tossed Pont the keys.

"Make sure you lock the door," Don barked unnecessarily.

"The last thing we need is for two country bumpkin police detectives to come to the big city and have their undercover police vehicle stolen. We would be all over the *Orlando Sentinel* and give a bad reputation to the Osceola County Police Department, not to mention the laughing stocks of our department."

They made their way through the parking lot and walked the short distance through the double glass doors. Across the street from the coroner's office was a strip plaza with a cell phone retailer, a fitness center, a karate dojo, and the Nail Bar whose sign boasted "voted best brows in Orlando."

To lighten the mood, Pont joked, "Maybe after we speak to the ME, we can get your unibrow manscaped."

A roll of the eyes told Pont that Don was not amused.

As the men entered the building, they offered their standard greeting.

"I am Detective Don Hannon, and this is my partner, Detective Mike Pontonero."

Both officers offered a cursory flash of their respective badges to the woman behind the presumably bulletproof glass.

"Good morning."

Detective Pontonero extended a nod in a greeting to the receptionist in the lobby of the Orange County government building, which was shared by both Orange County and Osceola County. This complete team consisted of the chief medical examiner, a couple of associate medical examiners, a few forensic technicians, a few medicolegal investigators, as well as the administrative support staff.

"We have been summoned by the medical examiner's office to review reports from Anthony Grasso's autopsy case."

"Yes, Detectives. Give me a moment to access the case."

The solemn woman with her hair neatly tied up in a bun had freshly French manicured nails and thick, full eyebrows enhanced possibly with a tattoo or brow powder. She was wearing a crisp white buttoned-down blouse with a starched collar and had a professional and dignified nature about her. Her well-groomed appearance and businesslike manner projected herself as strictly business, the no-nonsense type.

"One of our administrative staff transcribed the associate ME's autopsy report this morning. The chief medical examiner is in court right now giving a deposition. The associate ME has a few more items she would like you to pursue further from the preliminary report you submitted. Further investigation from your agency will help to determine cause and manner of death to conclude the final report."

She clicked away at her keyboard a few more times.

"The forensic technician will go over the tox screens projected sometime later this afternoon or possibly tomorrow. The tech will contact you as soon as it arrives. We have your information."

She looked up from the screen.

"They'll be able to review the results and explain the findings to you then. The lab is backed up currently due to the COVID-19 pandemic, so everything is in a rush, more than usual. He can review that with you over the phone. No need to come back so far for that one. This case has been assigned to Dr. Shirley Porter."

Both detectives glanced at each other and smiled, grateful for small mercies. Two more hours coming and going that wouldn't be wasted in a car ride.

Pont leaned over to his partner under his breath.

"She's the thin, older doctor, the one that worked with us with the Boy Scout leader that ate the poisonous berries. She also worked with us on the double homicide in the meth lab in Holopaw."

"I remember her well."

Pont knew exactly with which associate ME they were about to talk. They had, in fact, worked several cases with her over the years.

He added, "She's good. I really like her. She speaks plainly, and her reasoning is sound."

"Yes, she processes her work quickly and accurately too," Hannon concurred.

Dressed in blue scrubs from head to toe, the slender sexagenarian walked at a brisk pace. There were no formalities.

"Gentleman, come on back."

Trying to keep up, the two detectives followed Dr. Porter through the maze of corridors until reaching the destination where Anthony Grasso's body lay exposed on the metal gurney.

"This is what I wanted to show you."

Dr. Porter immediately got to the point. There was no need to review the case with the detectives. She presumed they were already up to speed.

"The victim had apparently been bending over when he was shot at this awkward angle from the side."

She used both her index finger and middle finger to indicate the direction without touching the body with her gloved hands.

"As you have already seen, the small entrance wound here," pointing to a hole the size of an index finger, "and the larger exit wound here, where it pulled a sizable chunk of flesh out of the side of his torso."

The two men recoiled as their eyes followed the doctor's spindly fingers to the exit wound. The gaping hole was roughly two inches but definitely no longer circular. It looked like a firecracker had exploded in a raw chicken breast.

The corpse had a whitish, blue hue and was difficult to get used to seeing, even for veteran detectives. After all these years, it was still difficult to view without gagging a little. The two men held their faces in an awkward, contorted position as if they were in pain somehow.

"The rib cage was shattered on both sides, and his heart was pierced straight through. The shooter was either very skilled or the victim was very unlucky. Do you have any idea what the weapon was?"

Hannon rendered the first guess. "A .270 hunting rifle?"

"Not bad. The size is similar, but no. Detective Pontonero, would you like to hazard a guess?"

He responded, "A .243 hunting rifle?"

"You are both on the right track. I believe it was from hunting but from a powerful bow and an arrow rather than a gun, though I am not convinced it was intentional because of the angle from which he was shot. A hunter would aim at the broadest part of the body for an animal, on its side, but for a human, the advantage would be heading straight on from the front such as his chest or from the rear such as his back.

"Our victim had his arms in a raised position, but he was doubled over. He was most likely working on unhooking his trailer from his truck or detaching his lights. In the dark, bunched over like that, it was unlikely that he was ever seen by the perpetrator.

"Had he been standing erect, his arms would have most likely prevented the death as they would be dangling downward, resting at his side. Even if he was standing with his arms crossed, his upper arms would have obstructed the path of the arrow at his side. The angle is downward slightly."

This time, she used a laser pointer to indicate the path left to right.

"I believe what we are looking for is an arrow, gentlemen. Either from a compound bow or possibly a crossbow but definitely not a recurve bow because that would still be stuck in our victim. It would not be powerful enough to exit the body."

The detectives looked at each other, processing the new information.

"There was no arrow found at the scene," Hannon reminded the doctor.

Dr. Porter informed the detectives, "I have been to the scene. Initially, we were looking for bullet holes in the walls of the house or in the car. Forensics found nothing when they swept the truck and trailer. The fingerprints found on the vehicle were Anthony Grasso's alone, our deceased."

"Do we have a time of death?" Hannon queried.

"The time of death is a window of two hours from 4:30 to 6:30 a.m. I recorded 0500 as the approximate time of death."

"It is pitch-black at that time and location."

"There was a streetlamp, but most likely, he was well obscured. He wouldn't have been illuminated because he was in the driveway, a good distance from the light, surrounded by a cover of shrubs, and blocked by his F250 pickup truck and large trailer.

Hands on her hips, Dr. Porter asked, "Have any of your people of interest, that you've come across, had any weapons like this?"

"The Kraus family let me look through every inch of their house, even the garage where they stored the hunting paraphernalia. They were the only hunters that we came across, and there was no sign of bows or arrows or even an interest in that," Pontonero answered.

"The people across the street…"

Detective Hannon paused while he pulled out his notepad to double-check his memory.

"The Washingtons had a handgun, but they hadn't lived in the neighborhood long enough to have cause to kill a man. I saw no bow and arrow while I walked their house. I looked upstairs, down-stairs, and through the garage of Mr. and Mrs. Washington's home. I retrieved a handgun that the husband admitted to owning, tucked between his mattress and box spring."

Pontonero added, "Forensics confirmed that it hasn't been fired recently on the *long* drive here today."

He allowed the word *long* roll off his tongue slowly to emphasize his displeasure and glanced at his partner at the mention of that ride.

"Neither seem like the hunting type. They recently moved to St. Cloud from Atlanta. They are still in the process of unpacking their belongings, but the only weapons that they could've used from my room-by-room search were the barbells and weights out in the garage. Both of them are fitness nuts and what Pontonero here would describe as 'granolas.'"

From the blank look on the assistant medical examiner's face, it appeared she didn't understand the reference.

"You know, they are healthy eaters, so *granolas*," Pontonero tried to explain it to the doctor.

"Yes, I understood it when Detective Hannon said it. I didn't react because I thought the two of you would judge me as a 'granola' too because I watch what I eat also."

Undaunted by her reaction or lack thereof, Hannon quickly shifted gear so as not to offend the doctor further.

"The only people we need to look at again for a possible bow and arrow collection were the neighbors with the weapons fetish. What was his name, the one with the attitude and all the knives?" Hannon asked, flipping through his pad.

Pontonero pulled out his notes and found the name first before his partner.

"Nick Mounts. You took pictures on your phone of his wall. Can you pull it up and see if he has any bows mounted or arrows?"

"I was just checking on that."

He puffed out a scoff as if he needed to be prompted.

Detective Hannon blew up the picture.

"Well, what do we have here? Looks like three good old-fashioned arrows beautifully displayed for all to see. We still haven't interviewed the wife because they had an alibi, and we had other priorities."

"We need to follow up on that alibi with the wife, and we still need to verify his story with the employees also," Pontonero responded.

Pont asked his partner, "Would you lie if your boss pressured you to?"

Pontonero stared back at Hannon. It registered that the alibi could be worthless even if it was corroborated.

Shirley Porter changed tack.

"Detectives, I encourage you to repay a visit to the victim's home. If it was an accident like I believe it may be, the arrow could still be out there. The blood on the arrow may have attracted animals from the preserve that could have carried it a few feet in any direction. Would it be possible for you to look beyond the houses, in the backyards, side yards, and even in the preserve area also?"

They both agreed that they would.

Dr. Porter pleaded, "I would really like to find that arrow."

"If it was intentional, the shooter would likely take the weapon with him," Hannon responded.

"It is my first speculation that the toxicology report will come back clean. Besides the hole through and through, the decedent was otherwise a healthy specimen. The death certificate must be finalized within seventy-two hours of our office receiving the corpse. We have already run through approximately fifty hours. That leaves us twenty-two hours remaining. I don't have to tell you that we need to get this done correctly, but time is of the essence."

She pointed to her tablet. "I can tick the box *accident, homicide, pending investigation*, or *undetermined*. I would much rather mark the box *accident*, if indeed it was an accident, as I suspect it may well be. Lack of evidence casts suspicion though, boys."

With a grave face, Dr. Porter slowly shook her head.

"Finding that arrow is paramount. I don't have to tell you what this would mean for the family. His family has so much riding on this."

She drew this line out slowly to call attention to its importance.

"If this is ruled an accident, the process of estates probate can be started. Mrs. Grasso can even make an insurance claim."

Dr. Porter used the woman's name to personalize the decedent's wife for the two men standing before her.

She continued, "The cause of death can determine if the surviving spouse or children are entitled to death benefits. The family can receive retirement benefits or social security benefits, have access to investments, just to name a few."

"Conversely, if you rule it a homicide, someone can be locked away for a long time," Hannon acknowledged.

"Exactly, and in Florida, while Jeb Bush was governor, Old Sparky was retired in 2000, but we still have the death penalty as you well know, so lethal injection could be on the table," she reminded the men.

"Well, an inmate could still request electrocution," Pont blurted out unthinkingly.

Hannon gently nudged the arm of his partner.

"Who would willingly choose the electric chair when so many things have gone wrong? You remember the heads sparking fire in the cases of Tafero in 1990 and Medina again in 1997? And who could forget the pictures that were released of that three-hundred-pound, triple murderer Allen Lee Davis in 1999? His white shirt was soaked bloodred from a nosebleed the chair induced. His groin, among other things, were burned."

Pontonero winced at the imagery.

Dr. Porter pulled the two men back to focus.

"As I was saying, the point is, gentlemen, lethal injection could be on the table if I rule it a homicide. A lot of unfortunate, unnecessary legal problems arise for the family, sometimes indefinitely, if I have to tick off one of the other boxes."

Both detectives took her point.

"That doesn't even begin to tackle the suspicion of gossipers. People they go to church with may turn their backs on the family if I leave any doubt. When I sign my name to this death certificate, I am providing my *best* medical opinion. I would argue that what I declare on the death certificate is more important than what I determine in the autopsy. The medical certification is prima facie. In other words, the proof of cause of death may be amended should additional evidence or information become available, but it would have to be rebutted in a legal proceeding. Sometimes, the challenges aren't successful. The family needs closure now, and I am swearing to the best of my *knowledge* and *belief* by signing my name. I am counting on you, but more importantly, the decedent and his family are counting on you."

"Message received loud and clear. If that arrow is out there, Dr. Porter, I assure you that we will find it."

Rather than a handshake or a fist bump to a blue-gloved hand, Detective Hannon offered his elbow. Doctor Porter returned the elbow bump eagerly. Detective Pontonero followed suit. It was a new norm for aloha.

Pont whispered to Hannon on the way out, "Let's get our brows done *after* we find that arrow."

# CHAPTER 26

# KRAUS FAMILY

*Morning of the killing*
*The Krauses' house*

"Dad!" Natalie shouted from across the house. "Mom said that you have to walk the dogs with me because Reed can't do it today."

"Oh, I just want a few more minutes of shut-eye," her father moaned as he rolled over and pulled the pillow over his head to shield his eyes from the unwelcomed, unnatural light that emanated from down the hall.

"It's time to hustle, Pops," the prodding continued.

She rubbed her daddy's back to gently lull him out of his slumber. This was a role reversal this particular morning as normally, it is her mother or her father that rubbed *her* back and hustled *her* out of bed.

"What's his excuse this time? Why can't Reed walk the dogs with you?" Mr. Kraus asked in an attempt to remain in bed as long as permitted.

Reed raised his voice to be heard from the kitchen.

"Dad. Please, I need the extra time to study the vocabulary for my biology exam. I'll do it tonight after dinner. I promise…without complaining."

Dad made a face at Natalie and raised his eyebrows like he really didn't believe the empty promise.

"All right, but you're robbing me of an extra half hour of sleep."

Natalie sprang to her feet and squealed in delight.

"Yay! Daddy's coming! I'll get the dogs on the leashes."

The sound of the word "leashes" sent the dogs into a frenzy. The dogs leaped over the back of the brown leather couch in one single bound each as if it was the first time they were ever allowed out of the house. This bad doggy behavior went unnoticed by the Kraus family. However, first-time visitors would get startled, be astonished, and belly laughed when witnessing it firsthand.

Mr. Kraus, meanwhile, threw his legs over the bed, summoning his courage to pull himself up and face the day. Mrs. Kraus peaked around the corner, bearing gifts. The rich aroma wafted in and put a smile on her husband's face. He wrapped his hand around the steaming mug of coffee, which greeted him like a warm hug. She leaned in for a kiss with the multivitamin wedged into her lips playfully. He stole the pill first, and then he took the kiss.

"I'll make some eggs with cheese and spinach while you walk the dogs. It will be ready when you get back."

Still in his pajama bottoms, he put on his slippers and found his dogs and daughter waiting patiently in the garage. The black lab was busy stretching his back in "downward facing dog pose," yoga style, at the bottom of the steps. The white labradoodle excitedly paced in circles just as happy as Natalie was for her daddy to come on the walk with them.

Playfully, he told his daughter, "Wait, let me get my headlamp so we can look for monsters."

As they rounded the shrubs in total darkness, a mental note was made by Mr. Kraus that Mr. Happy was not home yet. He must have had a lucky week.

# CHAPTER 27

# DETECTIVE DON HANNON AND DETECTIVE MIKE PONTONERO

*Two days after the killing*
*Lake Harmony Reserve behind Anthony Grasso's property*

Pontonero complained, "Man, this sucks. We should have some newbies out here stomping around in the mud and in the rain."

"At least it's not hot. I will trade you rain over mosquitos or heat any day of the week. Plus maybe the rain will wash away that huge ketchup stain you are sporting on your belly."

Detective Hannon looked up from the ground he was tracking with his eyes long enough to see the look on his friend's face when he noticed the stain. Don laughed out loud at the expression on Pont's face. He then returned to pushing mounds of dirt back and forth with his boot, to the left and back to the right, searching for the elusive arrow Dr. Porter so desperately wanted them to discover.

"Dadgummit! That's what I get for eating in the car. We need to stop going through drive-throughs and actually eat in sit-down restaurants."

"Time is of the essence, my man. Besides, you can barely see it against your dark-green shirt."

They were matching, both men wearing police-issued hunter green polo shirts with the county sheriff's logo embroidered in black on the left side of the chest. They wore steel-toed boots and cargo pants, easy for collecting items when investigating crime scenes. It was a completely different look from the suits they had on a couple of hours earlier when visiting the District 9 Orange County Medical Examiner's Office.

The conversation stopped as the detectives had started the search in the middle and were moving away from one another. Talking would have been increasingly more laborious with no walls for the sound to bounce off. So the search continued in silence, each of their heads trained on the ground and each being very methodical in their search.

On the car ride back from Orange County, Detective Pontonero did a google-image search for possible arrows they might be looking for. Of course, anything they saw they would collect, but to anticipate what they might find might prove useful. They were possibly looking for a thirty-inch or thirty-one-inch arrow. Hopefully, they would find the arrows that would be easy to locate, ones that were fluorescent colored with bright-green, orange, or yellow plastic fletching vanes. Pont learned that this was the part of the arrow that originally was made with feathers that directed the flight of the arrow in the right direction. Often, the nocks, or tips, were the same vibrant color as the colorful fletching vanes.

However, when searching on Amazon, Pont came across some arrows that would be much more difficult to find. These arrows were solid black.

It wasn't too long into the search before Detective Hannon was shouting for Pontonero, perhaps forty-five minutes or so in the drizzle. Both men were thoroughly drenched. Beckoning him over with both arms vigorously waving, he was standing well past the Krauses' house next door. Pontonero plodded through the muck.

"What did you find?"

Hannon pointed to a puddle and asked, "Do you see what I see?"

Pont laughed and retorted, "Apparently not. Where am I looking?"

"Right there." He pointed two fingers this time more emphatically and rephrased, "Under the palmetto bush, see the bright-green plastic?"

Just a small portion of the nock was visible. The rest of the arrow was submerged beneath the surface of the pool of muddy water.

"Yes! You struck gold, my man."

Pontonero gave Hannon a congratulatory pat on his soaked back.

"So you should go get it. You are already wet," Hannon teased with a broad smile on his face as they were both drenched.

"Finders keepers. But put on your gloves. There are tons of poisonous snakes out here, especially coral snakes and rattlesnakes, with all this standing water, maybe even a water moccasin," Pont cautioned his partner.

"Yeah, thanks for the pep talk," Hannon uttered under his breath. "I hate snakes," he added as he trudged through the dirty, potentially dangerous water.

Who knew what was lurking under the surface? He felt around the murky water until he bumped up against and successfully grabbed what he was determined to find.

He held the arrow high over his head as if he were displaying a trophy to cheering fans rather than just his colleague. And in response, Pontonero applauded wildly as if the car he bet on won the race.

Both felt the success of a good day's work, but it wasn't quite over.

"Seeing that you found the arrow and retrieved it in the muck, I'll wash up and then drive back to O-Town and hand deliver the evidence to Dr. Porter. While I'm there, I'll check on the toxicology panel. You can hang back at the station high and dry and write up the paperwork. I know how much you hate the drive.

"I am looking forward to a nice warm shower and a hearty hot dinner."

"Me too, brother. I also need to see a man about a horse."

That was Pontonero's subtle way of letting his partner know he had to use the bathroom.

Still riding the high from finding the elusive evidence, the need to investigate Mrs. Mounts didn't seem as urgent. Mrs. Mounts could wait for the team of two to regroup the following day.

# CHAPTER 28

# MINDY MOUNTS AND THE DETECTIVES

*Three days after the killing*
*One of the pizza restaurants owned by the Mounts in Kissimmee*

The bell rang, announcing their arrival as the detectives file in the small lobby. Mindy rushed to finish folding a pizza box, tossed it on top of the others, and circulated around to the front of the counter.

"It's almost lunchtime. Can I offer you a pizza? On the house, of course."

Mindy flashed a big smile and immediately warmed up the two detectives.

"No, thank you, Mrs. Mounts. Kind of you to offer. It was nice that you could meet with us on such short notice."

A driver returned and maneuvered past the detectives.

"Welcome back," Mindy stated to the driver.

"Is there someplace more private we talk?" Detective Hannon wondered aloud.

"I have a small office in the back, but I warn you, we can just barely squeeze in to shut the door for privacy."

Detective Pontonero nodded in the affirmative and motioned his hand as if to say lead the way and we shall follow.

They winded their way around the newly installed oven, and the hum of the pizza oven as well as the refrigerated chillers offered the privacy they were looking for. They passed the manager who was taking a call but smiled at them when Mindy introduced Esperanza as the manager of the store. They nodded politely toward her and continued until they reached the tight office that she promised, and it did indeed offer privacy, albeit a tiny space. There was another worker they squeezed past, but Mindy did not acknowledge him as he was busy feeding a pizza into the mouth of the grand oven.

"You're aware by now of your neighbor Anthony Grasso's demise?"

She nodded and acted like it was a pity even though the detectives already were made aware that she loathed the victim.

"Can you please state for our records where you were Monday morning?"

"Yes, of course, we had to install the new moneymaker."

She pointed through the small glass window at the oven. The window was presumably there for managers to keep their eyes on the employees while they dealt with money matters.

"Our old oven is out back. I can walk you out there to have a look when we are finished here. My manager, you just met, Esperanza Awilda Hernandez, was here too and helped us with the install. You may use the office to talk to her in private as I have a lunch date or meeting with my husband very soon."

"Yes, that would be most helpful on both accounts. Do you know of anything useful that may aid our investigation?"

"I really don't like speaking ill of the dead."

Her hands quivered on top of the desk, and she quickly removed them from sight and placed them in her lap beneath the desk that separated her from the detectives. Detective Pontonero side-eyed his partner to see if he noticed the nervous tell. He had.

"Nothing to be nervous about, Mrs. Mounts. Just be truthful."

"I am being truthful. I just have a slight tremble when I am nervous. An investigation into murder is a bit unnerving, you know?" After a sharp inhale, she continued, "He was an insufferable man. He cussed at children and old people. Anthony stirred up trouble in the

131

neighborhood, and at home, I heard from my boys that he even beat his son. He said the most vulgar things to people, but no, I don't have any idea who would kill him." She shook her head. "I am sorry I can't think of anyone who would have shot him."

"So you are aware he was shot?" one of the detectives asked a bit too accusingly, which jarred her nerves even more.

"Well, yes, my friends, Ron and Joyce, told me last night. We had a powwow about it because that is quite big news for our little hamlet. They said that you came over to search their house and one of you went to Ron's office."

They pulled their usual silence tactic on her so that she would be overcome by the quiet and spill information, but this method did not work on Mrs. Mounts as it usually did with most people, especially nervous people. She sat patiently and blankly staring at them until Pontonero finally broke the silence.

"Mrs. Mounts, we are aware of the bonfire, and we also know that you started the deadly game of imagining to murder Mr. Happy, aka Mr. Grasso."

With that, she brought both of her trembling hands to her forehead and cradled her head, knowing that the men could visibly see her frightened state. Her face was a tomato from blood rushing to her cheeks.

"He was wicked." Tears fell from her face. "The monster attacked my boys and other children when they were quite young. More recently, he came after the Washingtons and, before that, the Sundarams. We were having fun at his expense, but we are not killers."

She collected herself with a profound inhale. Mindy spoke slowly and distinctly.

"Anthony was merely the target of harmless, collective, neighborhood ridicule and pretense, nothing more than foolish banter. He deserved to die. He may have deserved to be slain. He may even have deserved to live a long miserable life alone with no friends and family to love but we," knocking on her wooden desk, "we have reason to live. We have reason to love. We have reason to live freely with our friends and loved ones. Not one of us has a reason to jeopardize our freedom, to risk incarceration or possibly the death penalty for his evildoings. Some of our children menaced him back, other neighbors moved away, the abused wives filed for divorce, his son moved out of his abuser's home, neighborhood men threatened him into submission, some of us ignored him and lived well. We don't commit murder to solve our problems."

Pontonero glanced at his partner and then back to Mindy.

"I will be sure to explain that to the dead man."

Just then, Mr. Mounts barged into the small office, deliberately forcing the door into the unguarded knee of Detective Hannon. The aging detective cried out in pain, massaging his knee, and shot an irritated look at the interloper. Nick witnessed through the glass window the emotional state his beloved bride was in. The despondent look on her face was solely the work of these prying old men. Nick Mounts never addressed the detectives. His eyes were trained on Mindy's eyes as he spoke sternly to the policemen. He wanted to punish these men. His body filled the doorframe.

"Are you finished here?"

Gathering his composure, Detective Hannon said, "Mrs. Mounts was just about to show us an old oven you dismantled."

"Esperanza!" Nick Mounts yelled over the hum of the noisy kitchen without ever turning his head or breaking eye contact with his wife.

She appeared through the window.

"Show these gentlemen the dumpster and any other thing they may need."

Nick was fully aware of Esperanza's commitment to the alibi she was to provide. It was obvious to everyone that he was in command of the room. The detectives knew he was not a man to be trifled with at this moment.

"I am taking my wife to lunch now. Feel free to speak to any of our employees. Esperanza is the manager."

His words were beneficent, but his voice was clearly agitated.

As the couple left the office, Esperanza politely spoke as if there was absolutely nothing hostile lingering in the air, and she was as calm and helpful as she could be.

# CHAPTER 29

# KRAUS FAMILY

*6:00 a.m., the morning of the killing*
*The Krauses' home*

"Thanks for breakfast, honey. I've got to get to the office this morning a little early to review my notes before the meeting. Who is going to wait with Natalie?"

"Reed just asked me to quiz him. It is crunch time," Mrs. Kraus responded first.

"Dad, I am twenty-one years old. I can wait by myself. I'm a fully grown woman, as Mom always says."

Mom glanced over her shoulders and smiled at Dad.

Reed interjected, "Dad, in middle school, I used to walk to the bus stop alone. You're coddling her."

Mrs. Kraus nodded to her husband in her most assuring way.

"Okay, if you say so. I am off to see the wizard."

Mr. Kraus smiled at the same *Wizard of Oz* line he used every day when he headed off for the office.

Talking to his daughter, he asked, "You want to walk out with me?"

"No, it's not time yet. I am going to brush my teeth and put on deodorant and listen to music," Natalie explained.

Gently griping Natalie's jaw, he said, "Don't be late. This is your trial run. If all goes smoothly, you won't need a bodyguard anymore."

She tilted the top of her head, waiting to be kissed by her daddy. He was more than happy to oblige, knowing he would never receive a kiss in return.

# CHAPTER 30

# NATALIE KRAUS

*Morning of the killing*
*Krauses' home*

"Bye, brother. Good luck on your test."

"Thanks, sis. Smell you later."

"Did you put on your deodorant?"

"Yes, Mom."

"Did you brush your teeth?"

"Yes, Mom."

"Okay, come give me a kiss before you leave."

Natalie leaned down to her mother and proffered the crown of her head for her mother to kiss.

"That's not a kiss. Come on, give me a real kiss."

"Really, Mom? She's never going to kiss you. Why do you have to go through this every time she leaves? By now, you should drop the guilt and just kiss her and be done with it."

"A mother has to try every day to get some sugar."

She directed this toward her son and then turned more gently to her daughter.

"Even when you are sixty-five and I am ninety, I'm going to ask for kisses when you leave. Bye, my sweet angel. Have a good day."

Reed recited to his sister their special little game, "Better shake, rattlesnake!"

She responded to her brother, "Gotta truck, fluffy duck! I'm out the door, dinosaur!"

Natalie finally slammed the door, a little harder than she intended. She cheerfully skipped down the steps, happy to greet her friends at school but even more so today because she was trusted enough to wait unchaperoned this morning.

Walking toward the streetlamp, waiting for the bus to pick her up, her eye was drawn immediately to the large bulky case leaning on the mailbox. She quickened her pace to open it.

She muttered under her breath, "They never let me take my turn. Girls can do anything boys can do, better."

She unlocked the case, clicking open the three tabs on the side. She explored it even though she knew she really shouldn't but also with the distinct feeling that she could get away with taking her turn, and Leigh and Reed would never be the wiser.

First, she placed the little black wristband around her hand. Natalie wanted to make certain she did it precisely like Leigh did. She placed the arrow on the rest, just as she watched Leigh do a hundred times before. Natalie clipped the arrow to the string next to the loop that looked like a *D* shape. She made sure to put the odd-color plastic feather up, just like Leigh said when he was explaining that instruction to Reed. It must be important by the way he emphasized it.

She firmly gripped the bow. It felt good in her hands. It was heavier than she expected. She used all her strength to pull back the string.

"Wow, this is harder than Leigh made it look," she said aloud to no one in particular.

Her hands were actually shaking. She didn't notice his hands shake.

"If Leigh can do it, I can do it. I think I can. I think I can."

Whenever she encountered anything challenging, her mother always encouraged her with this quote from her favorite childhood book *The Little Engine That Could*.

She tried to look through the scope but couldn't see a thing. It was pitch-black. All she saw was the darkness of the woods, so she really didn't even bother to look through the peep. She simply focused all her attention on the woods between the neighbor's houses. She knew better than to aim at the houses. She kept both eyes open despite not being able to see a darn thing.

With some difficulty, she drew the string back to her cheek. Just as she was about to release the arrow, she was startled by a noise she heard and took a step back to see who or what was behind her in the dark. Before she realized it, the arrow got away from her.

"Where did it go? Reed, is that you?"

No one replied.

All she could hear now that she was listening was the repeating sound of an opened truck door. She heard Mr. Happy's engine running, but she couldn't see anyone. The dense bushes that separated their properties obscured her view.

She whispered to herself softly, *I better put this up before Reed comes out. I don't want him to see me with Leigh's bow and fuss at me.*

Quickly and neatly, Natalie returned everything to its proper place. She leaned it against the mailbox where she discovered it. She felt very proud of herself for sneaking in her turn. She would keep this a secret and tell no one. She knew it was Leigh's bow, and he had asked her not to touch it. She knew he and her brother would be angry if they ever found out.

Even though Reed was five years younger, he had a way of making her feel like the little sister. She was self-satisfied to keep this secret.

The sound of the school bus engine rounding the corner made her heart sing. As the bus driver passed her house the first time, the driver vigorously waved at Natalie as she did each morning, to her delight. Just past the house, at the end of the street, the bus looped back around to pick up Natalie, and the loud double doors creaked open.

"Good morning, Ms. Lisa!"

"Hey, Toots, on your own this morning?"

"Yep."

"Well, get on the bus, Guss."

"Did you give your dogs a belly rub for me?"

Ms. Lisa played along. "You know I did."

*A fine start to the day*, she thought as she bounded up the steps.

## CHAPTER 31

# PHONE TEXTS BETWEEN LEIGH AND REED

*6:25 a.m., the morning of the killing*
*The Krauses' driveway*

Hey, man, come out.
I am pulling into your neighborhood
right now.

Shoot.
I totally forgot to tell you I am skipping first
period and catching a ride with my mom.

Don't worry about it.
I needed to pick up the bow anyway.

Don't text and drive, stupid.

Dude, I am sitting in your driveway.
Besides, I'm voice texting anyway.
I'm only going for first period.
Then my dad and I are heading up to
Georgia, getting a jump on the weekend.

    Sweet. Why are you even going to first period?

So I keep perfect attendance.
So I don't have to come to school on
finals week.

        I put your bow by the mailbox last night.

It's a good thing nobody stole it.
That thing cost nearly $400 with all the
accessories. My dad would have hunted
me.

      Relax, it was pitch-black at midnight after a
                    study session.
           Nobody comes down my street.
    Even if they did, nobody would have seen it.
          Don't slay any Bambis, killer.

They call me the Buck Buster.

    Hahaha, maybe that will catch on after you
                kill your first buck.

Good luck on the bio test.
It's mostly vocab.
At least the one I took was.
There is an essay comparing and
contrasting meiosis and mitosis.

    Okay, nerd, you better not get caught with
    that bow at school. Zero tolerance, bro.

Yep. I know. I'm living on the edge.
They'd never suspect me. I'm a Boy
Scout.
As long as you don't open your trap,
I'm good.
I got the bow. Later, bro.

# CHAPTER 32

# NITA WASHINGTON

*6:10 a.m., the morning of the killing*
*Nita's house*

Nita stared out of her window, drinking her morning masala chai. She could not have anticipated the good fortune to come. Surely, Diti, *Goddess of Revenge, Mother of Demons,* had smiled upon Nita with a powerful vengeance that day.

With Darius off to work, she was free to plot out her plan with what to do to the man who mentally tortured her parents and sent them fleeing to Calcutta.

This man, without a doubt, was solely responsible for the heart attack and eventual death of her father. She had nothing but time to figure out ways to drive this man mad as he had done to her own family.

Her poor mother was too frightened to live anywhere in the United States because of the constant, repetitive attacks on her family by this one man. Her parents explained that even if Nita and Darius had moved in with them, living directly across the street from Anthony would be too difficult for the elderly couple to continue to manage.

For years, he harassed the Hindu couple. Mrs. Sundaram did not believe it was isolated to one town or one state. Watching the syndicated news, they witnessed the rise of White supremacists, hate groups. Anthony Grasso simply won. The Sundarams were frightened enough into leaving their adopted home to return to India. Both her parents were convinced no matter where they moved in the United States, they would suffer the same prejudices and encounter similar threats and intimidations, and it wasn't worth the toll it was taking on Bapi's health.

Her only option, as Nita's mother saw it, was to return to India to live with Shyam, her brother, Nita's uncle. Too afraid to stay and live out their golden years in the United States, her parents left their Florida home to Nita, their only daughter.

Within a month of the sojourn back to India, her Bapi suffered his final fatal heart attack. It was just too much on the old man's heart.

*How should Nita respond to Anthony as he had when he tormented her parents? She battled with this in her mind. Should she take revenge and fight for her rights as Krishna taught? Buddha clearly would have desired for her to forgive and forget any wrongdoings. If she retaliated, Martin Luther King Jr. had suggested an eye for an eye would leave everyone blind, so she, too, would suffer if Nita sought vengeance.*

Nita did not want to jeopardize her own karma. It would take much reflection on how to handle Anthony. Did Anthony treat her family so poorly as a karmic reaction to something her Bapi did? Was it something her Ma had done in this life or a previous one? Or was this a result of some action that Nita, herself, had brought on? It could take time for karma to unfold without involvement from her.

The plans quickly altered as Nita observed Diti acting on her behalf.

Now it seemed Anthony was getting what he deserved, his karmic revenge.

From her window, still sipping on her chai, Nita noticed Natalie emerge, illuminated by the light of the streetlamp. Natalie, the tender, mentally handicapped young woman from Saturday's bonfire and who had brought her brownies, was fiddling with some sort of leathery glove and a complex, serious-looking hunter's bow.

Nita witnessed Natalie as she slipped the glove on her hand, standing under the solitary lamppost. The young lady carefully hooked the release aid on the loop, then clipped it to the arrow, and finally struggled to pull the tight string back. Distracted by the sound of the running engine, she turned around gracefully to see who was out there. As though being spun 180 degrees by Diti's hands, Natalie released the bow with the deadly aim.

The roar of the school-bus engine labored around the corner, signaling to Natale it was time to put away the gear and ready herself to board the bus. Taking off the glove and folding it neatly back in place, Natalie returned the glove along with the compound bow safely back to the mailbox where she had found them. By the time the bus had doubled back to pick up Natalie, she had her backpack on and was joyfully ready to greet the bus driver and her schoolmates for the day. Unwittingly playing her part in Anthony's fate, she would never have to suffer knowing that she had snuffed out the life of another human being.

Witnessing the entire event unfold, Nita Washington stepped outside to get a closer look when a teen pulled up, driving much too quickly in an old beater Jeep, with music thumping loud enough to wake the dead. While it couldn't wake the dead, it surely lifted the spirits of the dying.

Anthony must have been praying that the teenager would notice the blood and save him. Unfortunately for the dying man, the adolescent was too busy texting in the driveway next door to notice him languishing between the truck and trailer.

Diti, on the other hand, *was* answering Nita's unspoken prayers. Unaware that Natalie or anyone touched his equipment, the teen simply collected the evidence, jumped back into the Jeep, and sped away, bobbing his head in unison to the beat.

Neither he nor Natalie would learn their role in Anthony's doom.

Mrs. Washington remained unnoticed by the oblivious young man. Standing in her nightgown and robe, just a few feet away, hidden in complete darkness, she waited and observed until she could no longer hear the pulsating beat. She couldn't believe it. She savored this moment as she surveilled the life force slowly draining from Anthony Grasso's body.

He appeared unconscious when she finally approached the now limp form.

"Are you alive?"

She gasped in delight.

"I know you can hear me. Your eyes just opened."

She looked around to see that no one had observed her as she crossed the street and hovered over his huddled form.

"Where are my manners? We have never been formally introduced. My name is Dipannita Sundaram Washington. I believe you knew my parents."

She fumbled around in the dark until she found what she was looking for. The arrow lay near the garage door a few feet away from where it went clean through his chest, eventually resting on a patch of grass that pushed up between the bricks.

Nita's thoughts flooded her head.

*Diti just revealed to me how I can help get revenge for my family. I can still play my part in your suffering. It's so clear to me what I must do. I'm going to break up this sacred arrow and stuff it into one of the bags of the packing material. Later, I'll mail the broken pieces of arrow to my mother, one at a time, to India where you chased her away. Oh, what a fortunate turn of events.*

She ripped a large piece of elephant ear from his front island garden. Carefully, she used this plant to pick up the arrow and limit the amount of blood to get on her. With the arrow in one hand, she smiled and placed her finger to her lips with the other.

"That will be our little secret. Hopefully, Ma will return and live with us safely now that you're out of the picture."

She chatted away with her ill-fated neighbor. The one-way conversation made her almost giddy.

"There is no way that precious soul will be marred by your evil essence," she said, referring to the sweet-natured Natalie. "I'll protect her at all costs. I'll protect my good karma by helping protect the innocent."

The large leaf served as a barrier between the bumper and the bloodstained arrow. Under the cover of darkness, she loped back across the street to slip the now three smaller pieces that she had broken over the metal bumper into a wad of Bubble Wrap that she tightly wound. She tucked this into a small box. And this small box once more she tucked into the void of a slightly larger box. For now, she stacked the box in the garage among all the other boxes awaiting to be unpacked.

A few moments had ticked by. Nita glided back to the grim scene, bending down, hovering once again over Anthony, the way a small child inspects a bug on the ground.

In a singsong voice, she said, "I'm back. Did you miss me?"

With all the life he had remaining within him, he questioned, "Why are you not helping me?"

He coughed bewilderedly. Anthony was discombobulated and completely unable to comprehend why this crazy woman hadn't called 911 to report the emergency.

"It's not because you called us ugly names. No, no, I am much stronger than that. I was wondering when and if it would even dawn on you that I was the daughter of Suijit and Deblina Sundaram. You remember them, right? You tortured them the way I wanted to torture you. I wanted to drag out a torment equal in measure to your torment of my parents. But alas, it seems we may only have a short time together."

Nita took great pleasure in unveiling who she really was to Anthony.

"My parents were always kind people. They would never do anything to harm another living soul. They could have been good neighbors to you. They could have been your friends. My mother used to love to dance. Do you know that about her? She is an excellent cook and would have invited you to her home to have parties like they did with our neighbors when I was a child. Our neighbors up north were always invited over to celebrate each Diwali and share a part of our culture. You never had any reason to pick on them, but they were too afraid to have company here in this house, in this town, because of you. Harmony, huh!"

The irony was not lost on Nita.

"They are Mr. and Mrs. Sundaram to you. They had a beautiful stone image of Shiva on their front porch. I bet you remember that.

You marched up to their door and informed them that you would break off his raised hand if you ever saw that *voodoo hoodoo* garbage again. That's not even the same religion, you ignorant bumpkin," she corrected.

"You called them the most awful names, like a basic schoolyard bully. You made my mother a virtual shut-in. She was afraid to come out of her own house. I begged her to stay here. I told her we would move in with her and protect her from you."

There was a long pause of silence followed by a long released sigh.

"So no, Anthony, I will not be helping you today. I will happily call 911 after I am certain that Diti has sealed your fate and that you are absolutely dead."

She was momentarily startled by the neighbor's garage door, beyond the hedge, that rumbled loudly and abruptly as the motor pulled the door open. The unexpected noise jolted her heart. She concentrated to slow her breath. She tried to remain absolutely still. Mrs. Kraus and Reed Kraus emerged, reviewing biology definitions.

While Nita sat silently for a moment, still on her haunches, she overheard the son talking rather loudly to his mother.

"Eutrophication is the process by which nutrient-rich lakes transform into land. Phosphates stimulate aquatic plants that deplete the oxygen, which then choke the life out of the animals."

His voice trailed away as they packed into the car, just on the other side of the thick bushes. Anthony's eyes fluttered. He tried to shout, but only a gasp of air rattled through his lips. His own life was *choking out*. Nita slightly smirked at the timing of their discussion.

The garage door closed as loudly as it had opened. The car passed without pause. When they drove past the driveway unnoticed, she felt a weight had been lifted, and it was now safe to talk.

"It seems that we are alone yet again," Nita chimed in once more in her sweetest voice.

"The final straw broke when you dumped your garbage into their backyard repeatedly. Each time Ma picked up your garbage, it broke a piece of my Bapi's heart. My parents knew it was you all along terrorizing them, but what could they do? They eventually obtained proof from the security cameras they installed after one of your previous dumps. They thought about going to the police but were afraid the police would turn on them for being foreigners and immigrants."

She shrugged. "Even though they were legal and lived in the United States with a thriving business for thirty-five years, they still didn't trust the police to protect them. Until all the good cops root out all the bad cops, we can't trust them to protect us."

Nita shifted to stretch her legs and continued her quiet tirade.

"Who knows what lies you would make up. My parents were informed. They watched the news. If you were people of color in the United States, there is no such thing as a guarantee of safety. The police will never see the evidence that shows what a despicable human you are. No, today, the stars have all aligned, the gods have willed it, and justice has been dispensed. I will stay with you right until you draw your final breath before I report your death to the police. Not to keep you company or give you sympathy. No, I want to somehow facilitate your demise. I want to be with you when you get your just deserts. Unfortunately, for me, that looks very soon. You don't look so healthy, Mr. Grasso."

She checked for his pulse. She was right. The death rattle had been his final breath. It dawned on Nita that she had been talking to a corpse since the Krauses pulled out of the driveway. He missed her final diatribe. Now it was time for her to call in the emergency and feign her shock.

"911, what's your emergency?"

# CHAPTER 33

# POLICE LIEUTENANT CADE LA LIBERTY

*Two weeks after the killing*
*St. Cloud Police Department*

"Thanks for coming into the office. Shut the door behind you, please. Well, Detectives, do you have any further evidence or anything new to add on the Grasso case? Have you winnowed it down to one culprit?"

"No," Detective Hannon responded first. "I wrote every detail in my reports. I stand behind them."

He looked to his partner to garner support. Detective Pontonero pushed a thumbs-up gesture toward Lieutenant La Liberty along with a goofy grin.

"I have reviewed both of your reports. They look clean and thorough. It doesn't look like anyone will be pressing down our necks on this one.

"The assistant ME, Dr. Porter, notes the immediate cause of death. Cardiac arrest due to acute impact to torso, probable unintentional injury, most likely the result of a bow and an arrow. It goes on to provide the chain of morbid events. Rupture of the epicardium, perforated myocardium, excavated inner endocardium, cardiac arrest, which led directly and inevitably to death. Part 2 of the death

149

certificate notes a significant condition of deep vein thrombosis and pulmonary embolism, which did not result in the underlying cause of death."

"Huh."

It was more of a statement than a question. Pontonero rubbed the back of his neck.

"So she ruled out any guns, pistols, rifles, shotguns and knives, poison and medical injections?" Detective Pontonero queried only half jokingly.

"Looks like it," Lieutenant La Liberty said, nodding in agreement.

He looked up only briefly to see the faces of the two detectives standing before him until his gaze eventually returned to the paperwork in his hands.

"Your report from the forensic technician included the tox screen, which says that the only foreign substance in the system was Eliquis, which is a blood thinner, a medicine used to treat blood clots. That would have expedited the death to make him bleed out faster than normal. However, the language is deliberately vague. She must not have been comfortable using an exact diagnosis because she wrote *probable* unintended injury."

After reviewing the tox screen report, Hannon handed the paper back to the lieutenant.

"If you want to continue an investigation or have something more to add, we can drag this out as long as you need, boys. The associate medical examiner deemed it an *accident*. She wrote that it was a possible homicide only if further information was introduced, probable accident considering the proximity to the Lake Harmony Preserve and the frequent reports of illegal hunting in the neighboring woods."

Hannon shook his head no and turned his lips downward.

"We don't have any new leads. No fingerprints were found on the arrow you retrieved. There were no foreign fingerprints located on the truck or the trailer. No trace evidence. No new suspects have been identified recently, and the most likely suspects have all been vetted and have solid alibis. The arrow was found in close proximity to the site of impact. Having been soaked in a puddle for a couple of days, no further evidence could be obtained forensically from it. Based on her findings and your reports, I've got to say, fellas…"

He unfolded his hands and left them suspended open in the air momentarily.

"What is that look on your face, Detective Pontonero?"

"I see where you are going with this. You want us to close the case out and move on to other business. I would, however, be remiss if I didn't mention the two thoughts that are coursing through my mind."

"Okay, proceed, Detective."

The lieutenant leaned back in his chair and braced the metal arm rails as if waiting for bad news.

"First, the time of day. Why would anyone hunt at the crack of dawn?"

With his finger in the air, Detective Hannon said, "I've got this one, Lieutenant." He faced Pont and said, "That's when hunters hunt. They want to arrive before the animals are restless. They want to be in position before the animals are on the move. Especially deer."

He shrugged his shoulders with a Mona Lisa smile.

"My dad was a deer hunter. I went with him a few times as a kid."

"My thoughts precisely, Detective. Well done. What is your second concern?" La Liberty probed.

"Does anyone have any qualms about the fact that he was so hated by everyone? That he was threatened by so many people? Revenge seems like a possible motive to murder a man loathed by all."

"I have thought about that," Lieutenant La Liberty admitted. "Sometimes, justice has a way of working itself out organically. His karma may have caught up with him."

"Agreed," Hannon said, nodding.

Pontonero started singing John Lennon's song. "Instant karma's gonna get you. It's going to knock you right on the head. You better get yourself together. Pretty soon, you're going to be dead!"

Lieutenant La Liberty dropped a file and slid it across the desk.

"Okay, gentlemen, since you are officially off the Grasso investigation, you are needed on 192 and Pine Grove. A driver missed the stop sign completely and plowed right into traffic. It's a mess, and they can use a hand. Probably a drunk driver."

# SOCRATIC SEMINAR QUESTIONS
## OR BOOK CLUB QUESTIONS

1. If the weapon was disposed of, what evidence did the detectives really find?
2. Predict the killer throughout the book. Did your predictions change? What clues ruled out the suspects?
3. What is the theme of *He Deserved to Die*? Find the evidence in the text of when the theme recurs.
4. What are the red herrings of the story?
5. How was personification used as a rhetorical device?
6. What symbolism was used in Nita's dream at the bonfire?
7. Can you find any examples of irony in the book?
8. The word *schadenfreude* was used twice in *He Deserved to Die*. Can you apply this vocabulary in your own life or the world around you?
9. What clues did the author leave throughout the story for the reader to discover who the killer was?
10. *Esperanza* in Spanish means "hope." How did the character Esperanza provide hope to the Mounts?
11. When was foreshadowing utilized in the book?
12. What was your favorite part? Why?
13. Can you write three of your own questions pertaining to the book?

# ABOUT THE AUTHOR

Anna Ruth Worten-Fritz is a mother of two and resides part-time in St. Cloud, Florida (the setting of this book) and part-time in New Smyrna Beach, Florida. She lives with her husband of thirty years, her daughter, and two dogs. She received her bachelor of arts degree from the University of Florida and her masters of arts degree from the University of South Florida. She taught in Florida public schools for twenty-one years. She taught students from kindergarten to high school in the subjects of history, geography, and reading. Her final position was a literacy coach at Harmony High School, where she was inspired to write a murder mystery that would appeal to teens and adults alike. For a change of pace, she taught online for a year, teaching Chinese children how to speak English. In her spare time, she enjoys traveling to foreign countries and going on adventures with her friends and family and studying German and Spanish. She volunteered at the Adult Literacy League, teaching English to Spanish speakers and rocking babies for teen mothers so they may stay in school and continue their education. When her children were young, she helped coach Special Olympics in swimming, gymnastics, volleyball, and Challenger Baseball. This is her first novel.

CPSIA information can be obtained
at www.ICGtesting.com
Printed in the USA
BVHW081126160222
629188BV00002B/41